The Fig Tree
Murder

A Mamur Zapt Mystery

By the same author

The Mamur Zapt and the Return of the Carpet
The Night of the Dog: A Mamur Zapt Mystery
The Donkey-Vous: A Mamur Zapt Mystery
The Men Behind: A Mamur Zapt Mystery
The Girl in the Nile: A Mamur Zapt Mystery
The Camel of Destruction: A Mamur Zapt Mystery
The Snake Catcher's Daughter: A Mamur Zapt Mystery
The Spoils of Egypt: A Mamur Zapt Mystery
The Mingrelian Conspiracy: A Mamur Zapt Mystery

The Fig Tree Murder

A Mamur Zapt Mystery

Michael Pearce

Poisoned Pen Press

Copyright © 1996 by Michael Pearce
First U.S. Edition 2003

10 9 8 7 6 5 4 3 2 1

Library of Congress Catalog Card Number: 2003108659

ISBN: 1-59058-068-0

Poisoned Pen Press
6962 E. First Ave., Ste. 103
Scottsdale, AZ 85251
www.poisonedpenpress.com
info@poisonedpenpress.com

Printed in the United States of America

Chapter 1

'It's called the Tree of the Virgin,' said McPhee.

'Virgin?' said Owen.

'After the Holy Mother,' said McPhee severely.

'Oh.'

'It's a sycamore, actually. Not, of course, a sycamore as we know it. Our sycamore is a sort of maple. The Egyptian sycamore is a species of fig.'

'Fascinating!'

He glanced at his watch.

'Well, if you'll excuse me—'

'You will call in on it?'

'I certainly will.'

He certainly wouldn't. For he was going to Heliopolis and getting there was difficult enough anyway. The new 'city' was five miles north of Cairo and beyond the reach of trams. A road was being built from the British barracks at Abbasiya but was not completed yet. Even if it had been, there would still have been problems. Arabeah, the city's universal horse-drawn cab? Five miles? In this heat? The Effendi must be mocking. That left Cairo's normal mode of transport, the donkey. Owen was not enthusiastic.

Consulted, McPhee had suggested the new electric railway.

'It's not finished yet.'

'It's out to Matariya. You wouldn't have far to walk. Why don't you ask them if they've got a buggy going out to the end of the line?'

'Buggy?' said the man at the Pont de Limoun. 'Of course, Effendi! At once!'

Well, not quite at once. Second thoughts crossed the man's face.

'Tomorrow, that is. *Bokra*. Yes, tomorrow, definitely!'

'Why not this afternoon?'

'Impossible, Effendi. Some difficulties at the end of the line. Something to do with an ostrich, I believe.'

Owen shrugged and turned away.

A moment later the man came running after him.

'Effendi! Effendi! A thousand pardons! I had not realized that you were the Mamur Zapt!'

Another man, more senior, was rushing after him.

'A buggy, Effendi? To the end of the line? At once!'

'I thought there were some difficulties?'

'There are, Effendi, there are! In fact, we would be most glad of your help.'

'I don't know that I've a lot to contribute on ostriches,' said Owen uneasily.

The man gave him a strange look.

'Ostriches?'

'Wasn't it something to do with an ostrich?'

'Not as far as I know. There's a bit of trouble up there between the labourers and the villagers. And a man's been killed.'

❦

The man was lying huddled across the very last stretch of track that had been completed. Around him was a large crowd consisting equally of labourers and villagers, not, Owen was relieved to see, at each other's throats. Among them was a foreigner in a helmet, who looked up with relief as Owen approached.

'Monsieur le Mamur Zapt?'

'Oui.'

He looked down at the man.

'How did he get here?'

'I don't know. We found him here this morning.'

'This morning!'

It was already noon.

'I know! I've tried to get him moved, but—'

'He's not being moved!' said one of the labourers flatly.

'Just to one side. Then we could get on with—'

'He's not being moved!'

'It's taken all morning!'

'That's not my fault,' said the labourer.

One of the villagers plucked at Owen's arm.

'Effendi, the heat—'

Owen knew what he was thinking. In Egypt, bodies deteriorated rapidly. They were usually buried the next day. The body would have to be prepared, arrangements made.

A man pushed through the crowd. He wore the white turban of the religious sheikh. He walked up to the man and stood looking down at him.

'Pick him up!' he said.

'He stays where he is!' said the leader of the labourers.

The sheikh stared him hard in the face.

'God must be given his due!' he said harshly.

The workman shuffled his feet uneasily but held his ground.

'So must man,' he said.

'Look,' said the foreigner in the helmet, 'why don't you let him have the body? The circumstances can be gone into later.'

'It's the law,' said the workman.

'He's right,' said Owen. 'When there's a death in suspicious circumstances the body has to be left untouched and the Parquet notified.'

'Yes, but are the circumstances suspicious? Couldn't it just be an accident?'

'Accident!' said the leader of the workmen. 'This is no accident!'

'He could have fallen, couldn't he? Tripped over the track and—'

'Broken his neck?' said the workman derisively.

'Well, yes, he could!' said the man in the helmet. 'Couldn't he?' he appealed to Owen.

'Has the Parquet been sent for?'

'Yes, first thing. As soon as we got here and found him. I don't know where they are! Taking their time, I suppose, like everyone else in Egypt!'

At the back of the crowd a woman began ululating. From across the fields came answering cries.

'Effendi!' said the villager worriedly. 'The women—'

'Pick him up!' ordered the sheikh.

'Leave him!' said the leader of the workmen.

The crowd began to murmur.

'What do we care about the law?' someone called out.

'It won't help Ibrahim, will it?' shouted someone else, a villager.

The workmen looked at their leader uneasily.

'He stays where he is!' said the leader.

'You've got the Mamur Zapt here,' said the man in the helmet. 'What do you need the Parquet for? Isn't he good enough?'

The man looked Owen up and down.

'No,' he said.

Strictly speaking, he was correct. The Mamur Zapt was not the Parquet. All the same, Owen felt irritated.

'He's a troublemaker,' the man in the helmet said aside to Owen. 'That's what it's all about, you know.'

The crowd was stirring. Villagers and workmen were separating out.

The cries across the fields were getting closer.

'Pick him up!' said the sheikh.

The villagers surged forward. The workmen formed up in a line between them and the body. Both sides, Owen suddenly noticed, were armed with spades.

'Wait!' he said. 'There is a way of wisdom in all this.'

'The Law of God,' said the sheikh threateningly, 'does not wait on the Law of Man.'

'Break the law,' said Owen coldly, 'and you will feel it.'

'If there is a way of wisdom,' said the villager hastily, 'why not hear it?'

Owen guessed that he was the village *omda*, or headman, the man who was likely to feel the law most.

The leader of the workmen shrugged.

'Why not?' he said.

The sheikh hesitated.

'No one here wishes to offend the Law of God,' said Owen, 'nor that of man, either. For no man wishes to see injustice. And it may be that there is injustice here. For I agree with my friend'—he motioned towards the leader of the workmen—'that there is much here that needs explaining. On the other hand,' he continued hastily, as the sheikh opened his mouth, 'there are requirements of decency which must be observed.'

'True,' said the sheikh.

'The women have their duties.'

'Quite right!' said the *omda*, thinking he saw the way that things were going.

'But then,' said Owen, 'the men have their requirements too.'

'They do?'

'Yes. The men of the family, and those who have worked with him, will want to know that justice has been done.'

'That's right!' asserted the leader of the workmen.

'But—' began the sheikh.

'In the village, too,' continued Owen quickly, addressing the crowd and bypassing the sheikh, 'there will be men who say: "Let us proceed with circumspection, for there are dark and weighty things here."'

'Yes. No. You think?' said the *omda*, spinning.

'There speaks the man of experience!' said Owen warmly. 'And there will be others among you, leaders in the village, experienced, wise, who will think as he does!'

'So?' said the sheikh.

'So?' said the leader of the workmen.

In the nick of time it came to Owen.

'Such wisdom should not lightly be set aside!' he said sternly.
'Well, no, but—'

'Choose three men from among you.' That should take some
time. 'Let them sit with me and with the *omda*'—best to put him
on the spot—'and with the man of God'—that should take care
of *him*—'and then let us take counsel in front of you all.'

'But that will take—' began the sheikh.

'Effendi, the body—' said the *omda* worriedly.

'Rightly spoken! There is a need for haste. And therefore let
the choosing of the men begin.'

He walked purposefully aside. The members of the crowd
looked at each other hesitantly.

And then began choosing.

Phew! thought Owen.

Across the fields wove a column of women in black, ululating as they came.

∽∽∽

'So,' said the Consul-General's ADC, as they sat sipping their
drinks on the verandah of the Sporting Club, 'you referred it
to committee?'

'Instinct,' said Owen. 'My years of experience with the Egyptian bureaucracy have taught me that's what you do with a crisis.
Fortunately, the Parquet arrived soon afterwards and I was able
to hand it all over to them.'

'A pity,' said Paul, reflecting, 'since you were already involved.'

'Ah, but that was by accident. It's really nothing to do with
me at all. Not the sort of thing I handle.'

He stopped.

'Already?' he said.

'Actually,' said Paul, 'that was what I wanted to talk to you
about.'

∽∽∽

Salah-el-Din, the mamur of the new city, was waiting for him
at the gate of one of the few houses that had been completed. It

was a surprising house for an inspector of police, large, white-stuccoed and Indo-European in style. But the Syndicate had insisted on the house being in keeping with the character of the others in the development.

The new city was targeted at the very wealthy, who, apart from benefiting from the purity of the air, would also benefit from close proximity to the ruler of Egypt, the Khedive, who had a palace at Kubba.

The city was not built yet and it was pushing things to appoint a mamur this early, but the syndicate behind the development had requested it in the interests of community relations, which was very splendid, and had offered to pay the mamur's salary for the first two years, which was even more splendid.

They had gone so far as to put forward Salah-el-Din's name. Garvin, the Commandant of the Cairo Police Force, was normally against that sort of thing, but Salah was a bright young chap and due for promotion and they would need someone special for the job anyway. The Khedive could be relied on to make difficulties; and the Syndicate's wealthy clientele would certainly feel that they merited especially sophisticated policing.

Salah-el-Din, it was suggested, was just the man for the job. Unusually for an Egyptian, he had trained abroad, not, it was true, as a policeman but as some sort of lawyer (he had come unstuck in his examinations, which was why he had descended to become a policeman) and spoke French well enough to be able to liaise with the Syndicate (which was Belgian).

Owen knew very little about him beyond the fact that he played tennis. Rather well, in fact, as Owen had discovered a few weeks ago when he had played against him during a tennis party got up by the Consul-General.

'Where did you find *him*?' he had complained afterwards to Paul.

'His name was suggested by the Baron.'

'Baron?'

'The one we're sucking up to this afternoon, silly!'

Consulate tennis parties were rarely without political purposes. The Baron was the wealthy Belgian behind the Heliopolis
Syndicate. Wealthy financiers who took an interest in Egypt were
much to be encouraged.

A week or two later Owen had been invited to make up a
doubles at the Sporting Club. The invitation had come from
Raoul, a Belgian he had met at the tennis party and who was
something to do with the Syndicate, and the other two were
Paul and Salah-el-Din. It was then that Salah had issued his
own invitation to Owen.

'Come over,' he had said, 'and you can see how it's all developing. The tennis courts should be ready by next week—they're
building a big new Sporting Park. Why don't you come and
christen them?'

Why not, indeed? And Owen had been on his way the day
before when he had been so annoyingly diverted.

He made his apologies.

'Not at all, my dear fellow!' cried Salah-el-Din, leading him
through the garden and up on to the verandah, where a jug
of lemonade was waiting. 'It was all very nearly rather nasty, I
gather?'

'Not so much nasty as irritating,' said Raoul, already sitting
at the table. 'We lost a whole day! Actually,' he said, correcting
himself, 'it could have got nasty. We have the Mamur Zapt to
thank that it didn't.'

He gave a polite half-bow in Owen's direction.

'What was it all about?' asked the other member of the party
carelessly. He was, Owen gathered, the son of a Pasha.

'Trouble between the labourers and the villagers,' said Salah-
el-Din.

The Pasha's son sat up.

'Villagers?' he said. 'Have they been making a nuisance of
themselves?'

He probably thought the villagers belonged to him. Which,
until recently, they may well have done.

'No, no,' said Raoul. 'It's our own men.'

'Actually,' said Owen, 'it was a body on the line.'

'They could have moved it, though, couldn't they?' said Raoul, turning to him. 'From what I gather, that was at the root of the trouble. If they'd let them take the body away there wouldn't have been any bother!'

'They were thinking of legal requirements, I believe,' said Owen.

'They were thinking of how they could get the day off!'

'Put a body on the line?' said the Pasha's son.

'No, no, I wouldn't go so far as that. But make the most of it when there *was* a body on the line.'

'They're up to all sorts of tricks,' said the Pasha's son.

'Well, I wouldn't put it past them. We've been having some real problems with them lately. That's where we're hoping you'll help us,' he said to Owen.

'I don't reckon to intervene in labour disputes,' said Owen.

'What *do* you do?' asked the Pasha's son. 'I've often wondered.'

'I handle political things.'

'But this *is* political!' said Raoul. 'There are some agitators who've got amongst them and we want you to root them out.'

'The employers always think there are agitators,' said Owen. 'There seldom are.'

'There are this time!' declared Raoul. 'We can identify them.'

'We-ell—'

'Oh, I know what you're thinking. But we can prove it. There have been meetings between them and known Nationalists.'

'Even if there have,' said Owen, 'that doesn't constitute a crime. Nor, actually, does agitation.'

Raoul looked disappointed.

'I must say I was hoping you'd take a different line. This development is very important to us. And to the country.'

'Damned right!' said the Pasha's son.

'We've spoken to your boss, the Consul-General—'

'I work for the Khedive,' said Owen.

'We know all about that. As I say, we've spoken to the Consul-General—'

Government in Egypt was a thing of shadows. The formal ruler of Egypt was the Khedive and he had a government which answered to him. But since the British Army had stepped in, thirty years ago, to assist him to put down a rebellion, and then stayed, behind every Minister was a British Adviser and behind the Khedive was the British Consul-General himself. Government was a thing of shadows; but which was the substance and which was the shadow?

'Yes,' said Owen, 'so I gather.'

'Well, then—'

'I'll look into it.'

'Thank you,' said the Belgian, relieved. 'That's all we ask.'

'However, I must repeat: I don't reckon to involve myself in labour disputes.'

'We're not asking you to look into the labour side—'

I'll bet, thought Owen.

'It's the Nationalist connection that worries us.'

'The Nationalist Party is usually in favour of development.'

'Ah, yes, but it's not in favour of foreigners doing the developing.'

'True.'

'The fact is, Captain Owen—Gareth, may I call you—?'

'Please.'

'The fact is, we're not against Nationalism. Far from it. But we've been aware for some time that someone is trying to stop this development. And we've got a pretty good idea who it is.'

'I hope you're going to put something stronger in this lemonade,' complained the Pasha's son.

Salah laughed.

'After we've played!'

He clapped his hands and a young girl came out on to the verandah.

'Some more lemonade, my dear.'

She bowed her head submissively and picked up the jug.

The Pasha's son watched her depart.

'Who's that?' he said.

'My daughter.'

Owen was astounded. In all the years he had been in Egypt he had never been allowed to see a host's womenfolk.

'We try to bring her up in the modern way—having lived in Europe, you know.'

'Damned good idea!' said the Pasha's son, eyes lingering.

Owen reckoned she was all of fourteen.

She returned with a fresh jug.

'Fill me up!' commanded the Pasha's son, holding out his glass.

The girl walked straight past him and filled Owen's glass.

'Amina—' began Salah-el-Din.

'Don't take it out on her,' said the Pasha's son. 'I like a bit of spirit.'

Owen caught the girl's eye as she went past. Fourteen she might be, but submissive she was not. In fact, from the look she had given him, he was having doubts about the fourteen.

'I still don't like it,' complained Owen. 'I don't reckon it's my job. It sounds like a straight labour dispute to me.'

'Probably is,' Paul agreed. 'All the same, the Old Man would like you to take an interest.'

'It's not political.'

'Listen,' said Paul, 'if someone as rich as the Baron asks the Old Man to do him a favour, then it *is* political.'

'So you didn't go there?' said McPhee, disappointed.

'Well, no, I'm afraid not,' said Owen guiltily.

'A pity. You were so close to it. And it's a site of considerable religious interest, you know. The Virgin and Child are said to have rested under the tree on their flight into Egypt. In fact, according to some chronicles, Mary hid herself from Herod's soldiers in its branches. There is a tradition that a spider spun its web over the entrance to her hiding place so as to conceal her.'

'Really?'

'Interesting, isn't it? Echoes of both Robert Bruce and the spider and of King Charles in the oak! Extraordinary!'

'Fascinating! Well, I must go, I can hear the phone in my office—'

It was from someone on the staff of the Khedive.

'We understand you're taking an interest in the progress of the new electric railway?'

'A certain interest, yes.'

'Quite a lot of interest, we hope. His Royal Highness is very concerned that the line is not advancing as rapidly as had been anticipated.'

'I'm sure that the contractors will soon be on top of any problems.'

'Technical ones, yes; but what about the political ones?'

'Political ones?'

'The attempt by certain people to use the Heliopolis project as an occasion to advance their own narrow Nationalist interests.'

'In what way?'

'By seeing that the project is never completed. His Highness has asked me to emphasize that he regards the success of the project as a matter of honour, both his own, and the country's.'

'I see.'

'Good. His Highness hoped that you would.'

Owen had hardly put the phone down before it was ringing again. This time it was Muhammed Rabbiki, a veteran member of the National Assembly and an important figure in the Nationalist Party.

'Ah, Captain Owen, a word with you. We understand that you're taking an interest in this sad affair at Matariya?'

'A limited interest, yes.'

'But why limited? Important issues are at stake.'

'Are there? All I know is that a man's body has been found on the line, and that, of course, is a matter chiefly for the Parquet.'

'Oh, Captain Owen, I'm sure you know more than that! How did the body come to be on the line? Who put it there? And for what reason?'

'All these are, as I say, questions for the Parquet. My concerns are restricted to the political.'

'But, Captain Owen, what if the answers to these questions *are* political?'

'How could they be?'

'Suppose the body were a plant? Designed to have a certain effect?'

'What sort of effect?'

'I am sure I have no need to tell you, Captain Owen. But one thing I can say with confidence, that it certainly is not intended to be in the interests of the workers, neither the workers on the Heliopolis project nor workers in general in Egypt.'

'Aren't you making too much of this, Mr Rabbiki?'

The politician chuckled hoarsely.

'I'm just making sure that you don't make too little of it, Captain Owen. And in order to make *quite* sure, I shall put down a question in the Assembly from time to time. We shall all be following your progress with great interest, Captain Owen.'

McPhee stuck his head in at the door.

'About the Tree, Owen—'

'Look, thanks, I've got something else on my mind just at the moment.'

'But it's to do with the business at Matariya.'

McPhee came worriedly into the room.

'Apparently, there's been a development. There's a rather difficult religious sheikh in the village, it seems—'

'Yes. I've met him.'

'Well, he's bringing the Tree into it.'

'He's what?'

'Bringing the Tree into it. It's a Christian site, you see, of particular interest to Copts, but not just Copts, Catholics too. The balsam—'

'What the hell's the Tree got to do with it?'

'Well, he says it's not just an accident that the man was killed at that particular spot. It's within the zone of influence of the Tree, and—'

༄

'So, it's become an issue between Muslims and Christians?' said Paul.

'That's right. As well.'

Paul took another drink. Then he put down his glass.

'Political enough for you yet?' he said maliciously.

'First, I'm going to arrest the bloody Tree,' said Owen.

༄

When Owen got out of the train, the ordinary steam-train this time, at Matariya Station, he could see ahead of him the broad white track which led to Heliopolis. Away on the skyline were half-finished houses and men busy on a large construction of some sort: the new hotel, he supposed.

Nearer at hand, over to his right, a pair of humped oxen, blindfolded, were working a *sagiya*, or water-wheel. Its groan followed him as he walked.

Far to his left, above the mud parapet which hemmed in the waters of the Nile, he could see the tall sails of *gyassas*, like the wings of huge brown birds, gliding along the river. Closer to was the great white gash of the advancing end of the new railway. It was somewhere over there that he must have been two days before.

The track led through a vast field of young green wheat, away in the middle of which an ancient obelisk thrust upwards at the sky.

McPhee, he told himself, would have loved it: both the biblical landscape and the reminder of something even older, the original Heliopolis, City of the Sun, where Plato and Pythagoras had walked and talked, buried now, perhaps even beneath this very field of wheat.

McPhee was not the ordinary sort of policeman. His interests were in the Old Egypt rather than in the New; in the Egypt of the Pharaohs and the Ptolemies and Moses rather than in the Egypt of the Khedive and the occupying British and the foreign developers.

Owen's mind, however, was gripped more by the New Egypt than by the Old. For he was the Mamur Zapt, Head of Cairo's Secret Police, responsible for political order in the city, and the chief threat to that order came from the new forces that were emerging in the country, to do with nationalism, ethnic and religious tension, and the growing impatience with the traditional rule of the Pashas.

If it were not for the fact that the Old Egypt had a habit of rising up every so often and giving the New an almighty kick in the teeth!

Chapter 2

The Tree was in a bad way. It lay prone on the ground and although it was green at the top it was very brown underneath. Its bark was gnarled and twisted and much gashed where the irreverent, or, possibly, the reverent, had carved their names.

'That's why I had to put a railing round it,' explained the man who claimed to be its owner, a Copt named Daniel.

There was a wooden palisade all round the Tree. It, too, was covered with names.

'It costs ten piastres to put your name on,' said the Copt.

'Ten piastres!' said Owen, aghast.

'That includes the hire of a knife,' said the Copt defensively, brandishing a large blunt-edged instrument.

'But ten piastres!'

'Think, Effendi!' said the Copt persuasively. 'Your name bound to a holy relic for perpetuity! That will surely count for something on the Day of Judgement!'

'You don't think overcharging may also count for something on the Day of Judgement?'

'The Tree has many virtues, Effendi,' said the Copt, smiling.

'Evidently. But does it not, from what I hear, have vices, too?'

'That is a calumny put about by the Muslims.'

'But is there not some truth in it? For I have heard a man lies dead because of the Tree.'

'That is a story got up by Sheikh Isa. For his own ends.'

'Ah?'

'He wishes to drive me out. So that he can take over custodianship of the Tree himself.'

'But why would he want to do that? If the Tree lacks virtue? And isn't the Tree a Christian relic rather than a Muslim one?'

'It is a Muslim one too. As for the virtue, that would return if the Tree were in proper hands. Muslim ones. They say.'

'And what do you say?'

'That Sheikh Isa is a greedy old bugger who just wants to get his hands on the cash!' said the Copt wrathfully.

⌘

'The Tree is cursed,' said Sheikh Isa. 'Anyone can see that. Otherwise, why would it be lying on its side?'

'Old age?'

Sheikh Isa brushed this aside.

'The question is: *why* has it been cursed? And the answer is obvious. The Tree fell down a year ago. *At exactly the time*,' said Isa with emphasis, 'that they began to build this new city.'

'So?'

'Well, it's plain, isn't it? God doesn't want them to build the city. It's an abomination to him. So he cursed the Tree to show us his anger.'

'Why does he abominate the city?'

'I don't presume to know God's mind, but I can make a guess. It's to be a City of Pleasure. That's what they say, don't they? Now God is not against pleasure, but I think his idea of pleasure may well be different from that of the Pashas. Do you think he wants to see such a holy place turned into a Sodom and Gomorrah?'

'Holy place?'

'Not here,' said Sheikh Isa impatiently. 'The Birket-el-Hadj.'

'Ah, of course!'

The Birket-el-Hadj was the traditional rendezvous for the Mecca caravan. It was about three miles north of Matariya.

'Do you think God wants a place like that just where they should be beginning to put their thoughts in order for the Holy Journey?'

'Perhaps not. But, of course, fewer and fewer people are travelling that way now. They prefer to go by train—'

'Train?' roared Sheikh Isa, almost foaming at the mouth. 'Go to Mecca by train?'

'Just to the coast—'

'Train?' shouted Sheikh Isa. 'They heap abomination upon abomination! Shall we stand idly by when God's will is set at naught? Has he not sent us a sign that all can read? Does not the Fall of the Tree spell the Fall of the City—?'

⌒⚬⚬⚬⌒

'Why don't you just lock him up?' said the Belgian uneasily.

'On what grounds?'

'Causing trouble.'

'That's not an offence.'

'It bloody is in my eyes. Anyway, doesn't the Mamur Zapt have special powers?'

'He does. But it's wisest if he uses them sparingly.'

'I reckon it would be pretty wise to nip this thing in the bud. Before it gets out of hand.'

'You don't lock up religious leaders just like that.'

'Religious leader? He's a potty old village sheikh. Look, Owen, I just don't understand you. This is a very important job and we're behind schedule as it is, we've got to push things along. This business of the man on the line cost us a day and a half. And now you come along and tell us there's a problem about a Tree!'

'I'm just telling you to be careful, that's all.'

'Well, all right, we'll be careful. Hey, I've got an idea! If that old man is bothered about the Tree falling down, why don't we just lift it up again? Prop it up with stays? I could send a truck round, we could use a hoist—'

Matariya, although so near to Cairo, was in many respects a traditional oasis village, half hidden under a mass of palms, banana trees and tamarisks and clustered around an old mosque with crumbling, loop-holed walls and a crazy, tottering minaret. Probably because of the proximity to the gathering place for the Mecca caravan, many of the houses were pilgrims' houses, their walls brightly decorated with pictures of the journey to Mecca.

Against one of the houses a many-coloured tabernacle had been erected beneath which old men were sitting on a faded carpet. In the middle of the carpet was a *dikka*, or platform, on which sat Sheikh Isa, intoning the Koran. At the edge of the carpet was a pile of shoes. A blind man was putting his foot into them to try and find his own by the feel.

The dead man's house was just beyond the tabernacle, recognizable at once from the mourning banners. The mourning was still going on. Owen could hear the women's voices in the back room, less frantic now, resigned.

A man in a dark suit and a tarboosh, the red, tasselled, pot-like hat of the Egyptian effendi, was just about to go into the house. He saw Owen, smiled and waited.

It was the Parquet man who had come out to the rail-head two days before when Owen had been trying to prevent a confrontation over the body. They shook hands.

'Asif Nimeri.'

'You're formally on the case now?'

The other day he had been sent merely because he was one of the duty officers. He was young and fresh and new, which was probably why they had sent him. Anything out of town on a hot day was for the juniors.

'Yes.'

He looked at Owen curiously.

'Are you taking an interest?'

'Not really. Just making sure of some of the incidentals.'

'Sheikh Isa?'

'That sort of thing.'

The Parquet man laughed.

'I think he's harmless.'

'So do I, really.'

'You're not directly interested in the case, then?'

'No.'

Asif seemed relieved. Conducting his first case was problem enough without the additional difficulty of the Mamur Zapt.

'I thought that since I was here I would look in. May I join you?'

'Of course!'

They stepped into the house. It had only two rooms, the rear one, where the wailing was coming from, and the one they were in. It was small and bare. The only furniture was a mattress rolled up and stacked against the wall and some skins, not cushions, on the floor.

Two men came into the room, an old man, probably the father, and one much younger, the brother, or perhaps brother-in-law, of the dead man.

'I come at a time of trouble,' said Asif ceremoniously, 'but not to add to it.'

'Your grief is my grief,' said Owen formally.

The men bowed acknowledgement. The older one, with a gesture of his hand, invited them to sit down. They sat on the skins.

A woman brought them water and a small dish of dates.

Asif complimented their host on the water and Owen praised the dates.

'The water is good,' admitted the old man.

'The dates eat well,' conceded his companion, 'though not as well as the dates of Marg.'

'God is bountiful!' said Asif.

The men agreed.

Owen, used to the slow pace of Eastern investigation, settled back.

'Although sometimes,' said Asif, 'the yoke he asks us to bear is heavy.'

'True,' asserted the old man.

'Does our friend have a family?'

'A wife,' said the old man, 'and two daughters.'

'No sons?' Asif shook his head commiseratingly.

'The girls are still young.'

Which meant that the family would have to support them for some time yet. It would, but every extra mouth was a burden on the family.

They sat for a little while in silence.

'Are you tax collectors?' said the old man suddenly.

'No!' said Asif, startled.

'Oh. We thought you might be.'

'You come from the city,' explained the younger man.

'I am from the Parquet.'

The men clearly did not understand.

'I am a man of law,' Asif explained.

'You are a kadi?'

'Well, no, not exactly,' said Asif scrupulously. It was not for a fledgling lawyer to claim to be a judge. Besides, the two systems were quite separate. Kadis were concerned with religious law, the Parquet, after the French model, with the secular and more modern criminal law.

'Who is he?' asked the older man, pointing at Owen.

'I am the Mamur Zapt.'

'Ah, the Mamur Zapt?'

They had obviously heard of *him*. Or, rather, they had heard of the post. The position of Mamur Zapt, Head of the Khedive's Secret Police and his right-hand man, went back centuries. Only things were a bit different now. The Mamur Zapt was no longer the right-hand man of the Khedive; he was the right-hand man of the British, the ones who really ruled Egypt.

'What brings you here?'

'My friend has some questions to ask,' said Owen diplomatically.

'They are not my questions but the law's questions,' said Asif. 'When a man dies in the way that our friend did, they cannot be left unasked.'

'True,' said the old man. 'Ask on.'

'The first question,' said Asif, 'is why, after the evening meal, when all was dark, did he rise from his place and go out into the night?'

'I do not know.'

'Was it to meet someone?'

'I do not know.'

'Did he not say?'

The two men looked at each other.

'All he said was that he had to go out.'

'Did he often do thus in the evening?'

'Not often.'

'Were you not surprised?'

'We thought he was going to sit with Ja'affar.'

'Did he often sit with Ja'affar?'

The old man hesitated.

'Sometimes.'

'But when he did not return, did you not wonder what had befallen him?'

'Why should we wonder?'

'What, a man goes out into the night and does not return, and you do not wonder?'

'What a man does at night is his own business.'

Owen caught Asif's eye and knew what he was thinking: a woman.

'And when the morning came and he still had not returned, you still did not wonder?'

'We thought he had gone straight to work.'

'After spending the night with Ja'affar?'

'Yes.'

'A strange village, this!' said Asif caustically. 'Where the men spend the night with the men!'

The younger man flashed up.

'Why do you ask these questions?' he said belligerently.

'Because I want to know why Ibrahim was killed.'

'That is our business,' said the brother. 'Not yours!'

'It is the law's business.'

'Whose law? The city's?'

'There is but one law,' said Asif sternly, 'for the city and for the village.'

'It is the city that speaks,' retorted the villager.

⁂

'These are backward people!' fumed Asif, much vexed with himself, as they walked away.

'The ways of the village are not the ways of the town,' said Owen.

'I know, I know! I am from Assiut myself. That is not a village, I know, but compared with Cairo—'

'You did all right,' said Owen reassuringly.

'I should have—'

⁂

'Well, Ja'affar, you work late!' said Asif.

'I do!' said Ja'affar, his face still streaked with sweat.

'It is not every man who works so long in the fields!'

'Ah, I've not been in the fields. I work at the ostrich farm.'

'Ostrich farm?' said Owen.

'Yes, it's over by the station. You would have seen it if you'd gone out the other side.'

'And what do you do at the ostrich farm that keeps you so late?' asked Asif.

'I feed the birds. You'd think they could feed themselves, wouldn't you, only if you don't give them something late in the afternoon they make such a hell of a noise that the Khedive doesn't like it.'

'The Khedive can hear them all the way from Kubba?'

'So he says.'

Ja'affar removed his skull cap and splashed water over his face. A woman came and took the bowl away.

'So what is it?' he said. 'Ibrahim?'

'That's right.'

'He was a mate of mine. We used to work at the farm together.'

'The ostrich farm?'

'Yes. Only then the chance of a job on the railway came along and he took one look at the money and said: "That's for me!" I warned him. I said: "They don't give you that for nothing, you know. They'll make you sweat for it." And, by God, they did. He used to come back home in the afternoon dead beat. Too tired even to lift a finger!'

'Too tired to go out?' said Asif. 'In the evenings?'

Ja'affar was amused.

'There's not a lot to go out to in Matariya,' he said drily.

'We heard he liked to go out and chat with his friends.'

'Ah, well—'

'You, for instance.'

'He used to occasionally. He's not done it so much lately. Not since I got married and he—'

He stopped.

'Found someone more interesting?'

'Well—'

'Just tell me her name,' said Asif.

A man came to the door.

'Yes, he used to come here,' he said defiantly. 'Everyone knows that. And, no, he didn't come here just to taste the figs from the fig tree. There's no secret about that, either. What do you expect? A man's a man, and if his wife—'

'Did he come here on the night he was killed?'

'How do I know?'

'You live here, don't you?'

'No, I live on the other side of the mosque.'

He was, it transpired, the woman's brother, not her husband.

'She's lived here alone ever since her husband died.'

Asif asked to speak with her in her brother's presence. This was normal. It was considered improper to speak to a woman alone. Indeed, it was considered to be on the verge of raciness to speak to a woman at all. Questions to women, during a police investigation, for instance, were normally put through her nearest male relative.

The woman appeared, unveiled. This at once threw Asif into a tizzy. He had probably never seen a woman's face before, not the face of a woman outside his family. This woman had a broad, not unattractive, sunburned face. Things were less strict in the village than they were in the city and when the women were working in the fields they often left their faces unveiled. Even in the village, Owen had noticed, they did not always bother to veil. Sheikh Isa, no doubt, had his views about that.

She was as defiant as her brother.

'Yes,' she said, 'he used to come here. Why not? It suited him and it suited me.'

Asif could hardly bring himself to look her in the face. Although she obviously intended to answer his questions herself, he continued to direct them to her brother, as he would have done in the city.

'Did he come on the night he was killed?'

'Yes.'

'And'—he wavered—'stayed the night?'

'He never stayed long.' She laughed. 'Just long enough!'

'Jalila!' muttered her brother reprovingly.

Asif was now all over the place.

'How—how long?' he managed to stutter.

'How long do you think?' she said, looking at him coolly.

Owen decided to lend a hand.

'The man is dead,' he said sternly.

The woman seemed to catch herself.

'Yes,' she said.

'He died after leaving you.'

'Yes,' she said quietly.

'He left you early. Did he say where he was going?'

'He said he was meeting someone.'

'Ah! Did he say who?'

'No. And,' said the woman, bold again, 'I did not ask. I knew it wasn't a woman and that was all I needed to know.'

'How did you know it wasn't a woman?'

'Because it wouldn't have been any good,' she said defiantly. 'Not after what he'd done with me. I always took good care to see there wasn't much left. For Leila.'

'Leila?'

'That so-called wife of his.'

'Why so-called?'

She was silent.

Then she said vehemently: 'He should have married me. Right at the start. Then all this wouldn't have happened.'

∽

The tabernacle was now empty. The pile of shoes had gone. The square was almost empty. The heat rose up off the sand as if making one last effort to keep the advancing shadows at bay. The smell of woodsmoke was suddenly in the air. The women were about to cook the evening meal.

Owen wondered how late the trains back to the city would continue to run. Asif, too, was evidently reckoning that the day's work was done, for he said:

'Tomorrow I shall question the wife's family.'

They turned aside for a moment to refresh themselves at the village well before committing themselves to the long walk back across the hot fields to the station.

'It could be a question of honour, you see,' said Asif, still preoccupied with the case. 'The wife has been dishonoured and so her family has been dishonoured.'

'You think one of them could have taken revenge?'

Revenge was the bane of the policeman's life in Egypt. Over half the killings, and there were a lot of killings in Egypt, were for purposes of revenge. It was most common among the Arabs of the desert, where revenge feuds were a part of every tribesman's life. But it was far from uncommon among the fellahin of the settled villages too.

'Well,' said Asif, 'he was killed by a blow on the back of the neck from a heavy, blunt, club-like instrument. A cudgel is the villager's weapon. And, besides—'

He hesitated.

'Yes?'

'It looks as if it was someone who knew his ways. Knew where to find him, for instance. Knew he would not be staying. Knew him well enough, possibly, to arrange a meeting. That would seem to me to locate him in the village.'

Owen nodded.

'And if that's the case,' he said, 'you're going to have to move quickly. Otherwise the other side will be taking the law into their own hands.'

The trouble with revenge killings was that they had two sides. One killing bred another.

'Tomorrow,' promised Asif.

A man came round the corner of the mosque and made towards them. He was, like Asif, an Egyptian and an effendi and wore the tarboosh of the government servant. Unlike him, however, and unusually for the time, he wore a light suit not a dark suit and was dressed overall with a certain sharpness. Everything about him was sharp.

He recognized Owen and gave him a smile.

'Let me guess,' he said; 'the railway?'

He turned to Asif.

'Asif,' he said softly. 'I am sorry.'

Asif looked at him in surprise.

'They have asked me to take over. Why? I do not know. But it is certainly no reflection on you.'

Asif was taken aback.

'But, Mahmoud, I have only just—'

'I know. Perhaps they have something more important in mind for you.'

Asif swallowed.

'I doubt it,' he said bitterly.

He got up from the well.

'I will put the papers on your desk,' he said, and walked off.

Owen made a movement after him but Mahmoud put a hand on his arm.

'Let him go,' he said. 'It's better like that.'

'He was doing all right,' said Owen.

'I think he's promising,' said Mahmoud. He sighed. 'I wish they wouldn't do things like this. It hurts people's pride.'

Mahmoud El Zaki was a connoisseur in pride. That was true of most Egyptians, thought Owen, but it was especially true of him. Proud, sensitive, touchy—all of them qualities likely to be rubbed raw by the situation that Egyptians were in: subordination of their country to a foreign power, subordination in government, subordination in social structure.

And the wounds were aggravated by what at times seemed an excessive emotionality. For a people so prickly they were surprisingly tender. Excessively masculine in some respects, they were sometimes surprisingly feminine. They were never in the middle; unlike the solid, stolid, sensible English, thought Owen. He himself was Welsh.

He and Mahmoud knew each other well. They had often worked together and had, a little to their surprise, perhaps, developed a rapport which survived political and other differences.

They watched Asif set out along the track across the fields.

'You'll need to pick things up quickly,' said Owen. 'There's a danger of a tit-for-tat killing.'

'The man's family?'

Owen nodded.

'The brother especially. There's another woman involved. They think he was killed because of that.'

'Her husband?'

'No. She's a widow. The wife's family. Asif was going to take a look at them tomorrow.'

'I'll do that myself. I'll come out tomorrow morning. However, I've arranged to do something else first.' He hesitated. 'I'm going to talk to the railway people.' He looked at Owen. 'You wouldn't care to accompany me, would you?'

Owen knew exactly why he was asking that. Any investigation involving foreigners was potential political dynamite. Most foreigners doing business in Egypt were protected by special provisions of the legal code, forced on the Egyptian government in the past by foreign powers. No European or American could even be charged unless it could be shown that he had committed an offence not against Egyptian law but against the law of his own country. Even when a charge was accepted, he had to be tried, in the case of a criminal offence, by his own Consular Court, and in civil cases by the Mixed Courts, where there would be both foreign and Egyptian judges.

And those were merely the formal protections. Informally, there were jugglings for reference, disputes about nationality and the use of cases as pretexts for the assertion of national interests. In such circumstances the cards were always stacked against the unfortunate policeman; and especially so if he happened to be Egyptian.

It made sense, then, for Mahmoud to ally himself with the Mamur Zapt. It protected him personally against political comeback and increased the chances of successful prosecution. At the very least it meant that the Belgian-owned Syndicate would not be able to fob him off without even listening to his questions.

Owen was quite willing to allow himself to be used. Like many of the British officials, like, indeed, the Consul-General himself, he had considerable sympathy with the Egyptians over this issue of legal privileges, the Capitulations as they were called.

But only up to a point. The Parquet, too, had its political agenda. The Ministry of Justice was the most Nationalist of all the Ministries and the Parquet lawyers were Nationalist to a man. Mahmoud himself was a member of the Nationalist

Party. Might not the Parquet be seeking to use the case for its own political ends?

'Why have they put you on the case?' he asked.

Mahmoud smiled.

'Why have they put *you* on the case?' he countered.

Chapter 3

'There is this Tree,' said the site foreman doubtfully.

'Tree?' said the man-higher-up-in-the-Syndicate, Varages, another Belgian. 'What Tree is this?'

'I gather there's been some problem,' said the site foreman, looking at Owen.

'Is it in the way or something?' said Varages.

'If it's a case of compensation—' said one of the lawyers.

The Belgians had brought two lawyers. They had also insisted that the foreman could only be interviewed in the presence of someone high up in the Syndicate. It was likely that Varages was another lawyer. With Mahmoud, that made four of them. This meeting wasn't going to get anywhere, decided Owen.

'The Tree, actually, is beside the point,' he said.

'I thought you told me I had to look out?' said the foreman.

'That was because of the attitude of a local sheikh—'

'That awkward old bugger?'

'If it's a question of compensation—' began the lawyer again.

'Pay him and let's get the Tree moved,' said Varages impatiently.

'It's not—'

'Can we get the ownership straight?' cut in the other lawyer. 'It belongs to this old sheikh—?'

'No,' said Owen. 'It belongs to a Copt. His name is Daniel. But—'

'Ah, the ownership is disputed? Well, that gives us our chance, then. It will have to be settled in the courts. A Copt, you say? And a sheikh? That will be the Native Tribunals, then—'

'I wouldn't recommend that,' said the other lawyer. 'Not in the circumstances. Much better to get it referred straight to the Mixed Courts—'

'On the grounds that the Syndicate is a party? Well, yes, of course, that is a possibility—'

'Listen,' said Varages, 'we don't want to get this tied up forever in the courts. We've got to get on with it. How long is it all going to take?'

'About four years.'

'Four years! Jesus! Can't you speed it up a bit?'

'If the Syndicate cared to use its influence—'

'What would it take then?'

The lawyers looked at each other.

'Two years?' one of them ventured.

'Two years? Listen, two months would be too long! We'll have to do something else. Or rather—yes, that's it. Why don't we just dig up the Tree and argue about it afterwards? It wouldn't matter then how long you took—'

'Dig up the Tree of the Virgin,' said Owen, 'and you'll have the whole desert in flames!'

'Did you say the Tree of the Virgin?' asked one of the lawyers.

'Yes, it's—'

'The Tree of the Virgin?' said the other lawyer. 'Are you sure?'

'Yes, but—'

'Does that make a difference?' asked Varages.

'It certainly does. Captain Owen is quite right. The desert would be in flames. However, that is not the real difficulty.'

'Not the real difficulty?' said Owen.

'No. Not from a legal point of view. The fact is—correct me if I'm wrong,' he said, looking at his colleague, 'the fact is that, well, the Tree doesn't belong to either the sheikh or the Copt—'

'The Copt's put a railing round it,' said Owen.

'Who does it belong to, then?' asked Varages.

'The Empress Eugenie.'

'Just a minute,' said Varages, 'the *Empress Eugenie*? Of *France*?'

'That's right. The Khedive gave it to her. In 1869. When she came to open the Suez Canal.'

'Gave it to her?'

'Yes. As a present.'

There was a moment's stunned silence.

'It's still there!' said Owen. 'I saw it yesterday!'

'Yes. She didn't want to take it with her.'

'And it—it still belongs to her?'

'In theory, yes.'

'We could ask the courts to pronounce,' said the other lawyer eagerly.

'How long would that take?' asked the site foreman.

'Oh, about eight years.'

'I don't think we'd better move the Tree,' said Varages.

'I would strongly advise against it.'

'The French wouldn't like it.'

'They wouldn't, indeed. They might even, I go so far as to suggest, see fit to treat it as a *casus belli*.'

'Moving the Tree? A cause of war?'

'It cannot be ruled out. As Captain Owen will know better than anybody, the French have always resented their exclusion from Egypt by the British. They might see this as an opportunity to reassert their influence.'

'I don't care who runs Egypt,' said Varages, 'just so long as I can get on with my job. Which happens to be building a railway. What are we going to do about this Tree?'

'The Tree, actually, is beside the point,' said Owen desperately.

'It certainly is,' said Mahmoud.

ᘐᗯᑤ

At the last moment the Syndicate had made difficulties. It had no objection in principle to meeting a representative of the Parquet and answering any questions he might care to put, but it failed to see any reason, beyond the purely adventitious one of where the body was found, why it should be expected to answer questions bearing on the circumstances of the man's death.

True, the man had been part of its workforce. But the death had occurred off the company's premises and out of company time, while, in fact, the man had been at home and in his native village. The death was, surely, a private or domestic matter, on which the company could hardly be expected to be able to throw any light.

Nor was it reasonable for the Syndicate to be asked to make working time available for Mahmoud to question the workmen. If the death had resulted from an accident at work that would have been quite another matter. The Syndicate would have been glad to comply. But it had already lost a lot of valuable work time as a result of the accident of the body having been found where it had been and it was loath to lose any more.

Besides, if the death arose, as it appeared it did, out of private or domestic circumstances, what was the point of questioning the man's working colleagues about it? What light could they be expected to throw on the incident?

In vain had Mahmoud put forward reasons. The Syndicate's lawyers had merely raised further objections.

At last he had looked at Owen despairingly.

'I think that the reason why the Parquet has asked for this meeting,' said Owen, 'is that it is in the Syndicate's interests.'

'How so?' asked the lawyers.

'Because while the circumstances of the man's death remain undetermined, all sorts of stories are getting around. He is concerned that some of these could have an effect on your workforce.'

It was then that the foreman had mentioned the Tree and they had begun on their detour.

'The Tree,' said Owen, perspiring and making one last valiant attempt, '*is not in the way. You do not have to move it.* In itself it is nothing. It is the way it might be used that is important.'

'To create mischief, you mean?' said the foreman.

'We certainly wouldn't want that,' said Varages, frowning. He glanced at the lawyers.

'What do we have to lose by letting him ask questions?'

'I think we should maintain our position,' one of them said. 'Strictly speaking, it is nothing to do with us. There is nothing that points to a connection between the man's death and the railway.'

'Oh, yes, there is,' said Mahmoud. 'We have found sand in the man's clothes and superficial lesions consistent with the body having been dragged. We do not think he was killed at the place where he was found. He was killed somewhere else and dragged there. And the question is why? The answer, surely, is to make precisely the connection between the killing and the railway that you deny exists.'

⌒⚮

'The money is good,' conceded the labourers.

'But the work is hard.'

'Heavy, is it?' said Mahmoud sympathetically.

'It's more that they keep you going.'

'They keep you going in the fields,' said one of the men.

'Yes. But it's at a sensible pace. On this job they make you go faster than you'd like.'

'That's because they want to get it finished. The Khedive, they say, has fixed the day he wants to travel on it.'

'Why can't he wait a bit?'

'He's got some big do on, I expect.'

'Well, if he wants to travel to the city, why can't he go by coach and horses, the way he's always done?'

'He's in a hurry, I suppose.'

'All he needs to do is set out earlier. Then he'd get there at the same time.'

'Ah, but that's not it. Speed's the thing today.'

'Well, I don't see why we need it.'

'You're a man of the past, Abdul. Egypt's bursting into the future. Or so they say.'

'Well, I wish they'd burst without me. There's no point in working this hard. It's worse than when they had the *curbash*.'

The *curbash* was the heavy whip the Pashas had used to force labour. One of the first acts of the British when they arrived had been to abolish it.

'You wouldn't want the *curbash* back, would you?'

'I don't reckon it'd make much difference.'

'I reckon you'd feel the difference!'

'*Curbash*, money, it's all the same,' remarked another of the labourers. 'It's all a whip held over the head of the poor.'

Mahmoud had been allowed to address them during their break. This was another bone of contention. It was usual in Egypt to work till early in the afternoon and then, if you were an office worker or a labourer, stop for the day. Shopkeepers would work again in the evening when it became cooler. The Syndicate, however, had insisted that the workforce on the railway work through till late afternoon, stopping for a brief break at noon when the sun was at its hottest.

The men were sitting in the shade now, eating their bread and onions.

'Ibrahim found the work hard, so they say,' said Owen.

The leader of the workmen looked at him.

'Do they?'

'Yes. In the village. They say he used to get home too tired to do anything.'

'He used to do his share.'

'It's not entirely true, though. There was a woman he used to go to.'

'Was there?'

'He didn't speak to you about it?'

'No.'

'I expect he saved a bit for that,' said one of the workmen. 'You'd do that, wouldn't you, Abdul?'

'I bet he'd work fast enough then,' said another of the men. 'There'd be no need for someone to be standing over him with the *curbash* when it comes to that kind of work!'

There was a general laugh.

'Why wouldn't you let them move the body?' Mahmoud asked the leader.

'He was murdered, wasn't he? You could see it. His neck was broken.'

'You wanted the Parquet to take a look at it?'

'Yes.'

'Why?'

'That's what they're supposed to do, aren't they?' retorted the man.

Which was certainly true. Only it was a little surprising that the man should be so punctilious. Few Egyptians would have been. The Parquet was—in Egyptian terms—relatively new, having been created only some thirty years before when the government, anxious to introduce a modern legal system, had simply translated the French Penal Code and adopted it and French legal procedure lock, stock and barrel. Many Egyptians still harked back to the system which had preceded it and which had prevailed for centuries, a system of village watchmen, *ghaffirs*, and in which the local mudir, or governor, was judge, jury and, frequently, executioner. The Mamur Zapt had been part of that system, which accounts for the fact that the Matariya villagers had heard of him but not of the Parquet.

Yet here was someone, ordinary labourer and probably a villager, invoking the absolute letter of the—for many Egyptians—still newish law!

It was a small thing, perhaps, but it set Owen's mind wondering. He knew little about employment law (and was damned sure that very few Egyptians did) and not much about labour disputes. Maybe it was different in the more modern industries.

Maybe the workers' leaders there did know something about the modern legal system. Maybe that was why the workmen, very sensibly, chose them.

Perhaps he was making too much of it. He looked at the workmen's leader. He was a youngish man in his thirties, with a thin, sharp face and a wiry body. He was certainly intelligent.

The doubt began to niggle at Owen's mind again. Too intelligent? He did not know what the workmen in Egypt's newer industries—the railways were, of course, one of Egypt's newer industries—were like but suspected that they might well be sharper than the average. But that would surely be true only of the more skilled trades, the engine drivers and signalmen and repairmen. It wouldn't necessarily be true of the labourers working on the track.

He was probably making too much of this. Only the Belgians had spoken of agitators, and he had dismissed it as the kind of thing foreign contractors would say. And so far he had seen absolutely no sign of this man being an agitator in their sense. He had directed attention to a body, that was all, and insisted that the due process of the law should be observed. Nothing wrong with that; it was just that in Egypt, a country of many murders and much casualness about death, it was a bit unusual.

He reproached himself. A man did exactly as he was supposed to do and it struck him as odd! What were things coming to!

The niggle, however, remained. What it came down to was, why had the man done it? Normal zeal for the public good? Compassion for the dead man, anger at the killing of a friend? Or could it be, could it just be, that someone saw in the death an opportunity to exploit the situation for their own ends, that the Khedive's charges of political manipulation on the part of the Nationalists were not entirely without foundation?

The men finished their break and went back to their work. Mahmoud, lunchless, set out for the village. He was probably the only man in the Parquet, and, possibly, Cairo, who reckoned to work through the heat of the day.

Owen took a buggy back to the Pont de Limoun and then an arabeah up to the Ismailiya Quarter, where, among the 'butterfly shops', he hoped to find Zeinab.

The 'butterfly shops' were open only in the season and were kept by dressmakers, milliners and purveyors of general unnecessaries who had come over from Paris specifically for the occasion. Fashionable Egypt was oriented heavily towards Paris, and the goods were the latest in the Paris shops. They were also the most expensive in the Paris shops. They were also the most expensive in the Paris shops and Owen frequently wondered what Zeinab was doing in them. She received an allowance from her father, a wealthy—or so she claimed—Pasha. He denied it, but then these things, thought Owen, were relative. A dress from one of the 'butterfly shops', which cost more than Owen's pay for the whole year, probably seemed like nothing to him. He could deny his daughter, his illegitimate child by his favourite courtesan, nothing. Not that it would have done much good if he had, she would simply have gone ahead all the same, bought it and charged it to his account.

Owen walked into the most likely shop and stood dazed and uncomprehending among the dresses. When it came to shopping, Zeinab reckoned he was good for lunch and not much else.

Yes, said the assistant, she was in the shop. She was trying on a dress and would be with him shortly.

'*Monsieur désire une boisson, peut-être?*' said the assistant.

Yes, Monsieur did *désire une boisson*, and stood sipping it while he waited for Zeinab.

Several other assistants were in the shop, ladies of considerable beauty and indeterminate nationality and all of them dressed in black. Nearly all of them wore veils, in deference to Muslim susceptibilities. Not too much deference; the veils were thin and filmy and suggested as much as they concealed.

There were, however, some women in traditional dress, wearing long, black, shapeless robes which came down to their feet and long veils which covered their head—the hair was a particularly erotic zone for Arabs—and came down to their waists. They stood incongruously among the skimpy and revealing European fashions, apparently as out of place as Owen himself.

One of them had a young girl with her, dressed not, however, in the traditional clothes but in something straight from Paris. The dress suggested youthfulness, childishness, almost, but the figure beneath was far from childish. Owen was still trying to work it out when she turned and looked at him.

Like the other women, she wore a veil, only this was neither the traditional one of her mother nor the usual Parisian one, but a Turkish one which covered the lower part of the face and revealed the eyes. Above the veil her eyes looked at Owen warmly and with recognition.

Salah-el-Din came into view, accompanied by the man he had introduced Owen to the other day, the Pasha's son.

'Captain Owen! What a pleasure! You have met Malik, of course.'

They shook hands.

'We can go there together,' said Malik.

Where was it that they might be going? The only other engagement that Owen had that day, so far as he could remember, was a routine meeting about an application for a gambling licence, and the only reason why he remembered it was that, unusually for Cairo, it was being held in the afternoon.

'My wife; my daughter, whom you met, if you remember.'

The mother muttered a polite greeting in Arabic. The daughter advanced on Owen with outstretched hand.

'*Enchanté, monsieur! C'est un très grand plaisir*—'

'A charming dress, don't you think? It's important to hit the right note—'

'You could try it a bit shorter,' said Malik.

Salah laughed, unoffended.

'You would think that!' he said.

The mother gave her head a decided shake.

'How about a drink?' Malik said to Owen.

'I'm afraid not,' said Owen, seeing Zeinab, tall, slim and elegant, sweep down the stairs at the back. 'I've a previous engagement.'

'Don't blame you,' said Malik, following the direction of his eyes.

Zeinab came towards them. Owen was jealously pleased that she wore a veil, a French-style one that covered all her face except for the sharp, rather beaky chin. Zeinab's father always claimed that there was some Bedouin blood in the family, although he was not entirely sure how it got there.

'Greek?' said Malik. 'Not Circassian, anyway. You ought to try Circassian.'

Zeinab walked on past them. Owen caught up with her just as she went through the doors.

'I don't like your friends,' she said.

'They're not exactly my friends. One of them's the new mamur out at Heliopolis.'

'Who's the girl?'

'His daughter. I can't figure her out,' admitted Owen.

'I can!'

Zeinab was silent for a moment. Then she said:

'How can a mamur afford to shop at Anton's?'

'That's what I'm wondering,' said Owen.

'I shall tell Anton that he needs to be more selective in his clientele. He can start by throwing out that other man.'

'Malik? He's a Pasha's son!'

'Good!' said Zeinab gleefully. 'In that case I shall certainly ask Anton to throw him out!'

~

Owen was a little taken aback when he returned to his office to find that the venue for his meeting had been changed. It was now to be held at the Savoy Hotel, which was roughly where he had just come from. His meetings were not normally held at the Savoy Hotel, but he had hopes that this might create a precedent.

At the meeting were a representative of the Ministry of Justice, McPhee, the Deputy Commandment of Police, two lawyers and Malik appearing for the appellants, and himself, and the subject of the meeting was an application to open new premises under the licensing laws.

Or, rather, not quite an application.

'A formal application will be made later,' said one of the lawyers, smiling. 'At this stage all we are doing is testing the ground. We are seeking to establish whether there would be any objection *in principle* to an application such as ours.'

'The government's policy is to restrict the number of gambling houses,' said McPhee severely.

'And quite rightly, too. There are far too many low dens where the practices are, frankly, far from commendable. Our application is not of that sort. It relates to the opening of a casino in the Palace Hotel at Heliopolis.'

'Palace Hotel?' said McPhee, puzzled. 'There isn't one!'

'It's being built.'

The man from the Ministry of Justice, an Egyptian, looked at his papers.

'A casino wasn't mentioned in the original planning application,' he said.

'Well, no. It has only recently come home to us how attractive an additional amenity it would be.'

'It's the government's policy not to allow new premises to be opened,' said McPhee.

'But surely that only applies to Cairo proper, where there is already too great an abundance of such places? We are talking about the New Heliopolis, where there isn't even one at the moment!'

'It is a general restriction,' said the man from the Ministry of Justice.

'But how can it apply to a place like the New Heliopolis, which wasn't even projected when the legislation was framed?'

'The legislation covers future development.'

'I put the question because of the special character of the Heliopolis development. It is to be a City of Pleasure. That was stated explicitly at the stage of the initial planning application. I would suggest that approval of the initial concept implies approach of consequent developments.'

'I would challenge the view that a casino is a consequent development,' said Owen. 'Amenities in general, yes, a casino in particular, no.'

'But I think you have to have regard to other developments: the racetrack—'

'God, yes!' said Malik.

'—which is an important feature of the new sporting complex. You can hardly have a racetrack without gambling!'

'God, no!' said Malik.

'Thank you, Mr Hosnani. I argue firstly, that implicit in the approval of the racetrack was approval of related gambling facilities—'

'But they're not related!' protested Owen.

'It's all the same thing,' said Malik. 'What you lose on the swings, you lose on the roundabouts.'

'A casino is quite different!'

'Not in character, Captain Owen. And that is really my point: the character of Heliopolis as a City of Pleasure.'

'I'm all for pleasure,' said Malik.

'Thank you, Mr Hosnani. We are not talking about some low, vicious den but about a tasteful, discreet, modest development in a major hotel—'

'Modest?' said the man from the Ministry of Justice, studying his papers. 'It's gigantic!'

'There's another point about character,' said Owen. 'Have you thought about the proximity to the gathering place for the Mecca caravan?'

'Ah, Captain Owen!' said the lawyer, smiling. 'I think you're a little out of date, you know. We all go by train now.'

'Do we?' said Malik, startled.

'No,' said Owen. 'Not everyone. There's still a caravan.'

'For how long? No, Captain Owen—' the lawyer smiled and shook his head—'we must look to the future. And Heliopolis is the future.'

'I think we have to have regard to local religious feeling,' said Owen.

The other lawyer intervened.

'With the greatest respect,' he said, 'I'm not sure that the Mamur Zapt is the best interpreter of religious feeling.'

'No?' said the man from the Ministry of Justice.

'No. There is, in fact, very considerable local support for the venture. I would go so far as to say that it has captured the imagination of the local populace. As Mr Hosnani, here, is in a position to testify.'

'You're damned right,' said Malik. 'We're all in favour. Can't wait to get started.'

'With the greatest respect,' said Owen, 'I doubt whether Mr Hosnani *is* in a position to testify; not, at least, as far as the views of the ordinary man are concerned.'

'I'm a local resident, aren't I?' said Malik indignantly.

Chapter 4

A few people stood around but, compared with what it would have been in the city, it was nothing. In the city, the crowd would have filled the street. Here, an old man looked up while watering his goats, some women with jugs on their heads paused on their way to the well, men stooping in the fields looked as they straightened their backs for a moment. One or two villagers had come out to see what was going on; and beside the Tree, Daniel, the Copt, stood vigilant, hoping somehow to turn this into a bargain.

The space in front of the Tree was roped off and some men in police tunics and military-style tarbooshes were crouched down examining the ground. Despite the sun, which made the sand so hot that it almost burned the hand, they had bare feet; and although they looked not very different from ordinary city policemen, they were in fact men of the desert. They were the police force's professional trackers.

Some of their achievements were legendary. On one occasion some goods had been thrown out of a train in the middle of the desert. Accomplices waiting on camels had taken them to Port Said, over a hundred miles away; where the trackers had found them in the market, identifying them by camel track alone.

'I had thought it might be too late,' said Mahmoud, 'and, of course, the ground at the railhead was very disturbed. There had been so many people milling about that first day. But out beyond the disturbed ground they were able to pick up the trail.

It was partly the different kinds of sand they found on the body, but then they also found tracks.'

'And it led back to here?' said Owen.

'Yes. This is where he was killed.'

One of the trackers looked up and pointed to a patch of ground.

'He fell here?'

Owen bent down and looked closely. He didn't really expect to see anything and he wasn't disappointed. However, he knew the trackers well enough to believe them. On second thoughts, that might be a slight declivity.

The tracker pointed to one side of it and made smoothing movements with his hand. Yes, you could argue that something had been dragged. He stood up and, beckoning to Owen to follow him, set off across the desert, pointing to the ground.

To him it was as plain as a pikestaff. To Owen it was the next best thing to invisible; only, from time to time, the tracker bent down and showed him marks which he certainly could see. The difficult thing was pulling the marks together to establish the trail as a whole. This was where, presumably, the different types of sand came in. Here again, to Owen the differences were practically indistinguishable. To the trackers they leaped out a mile.

The tracker led him across the desert to the railway, where some of the men he and Mahmoud had talked to the previous day were laying the track. New lengths had been added. The tracker disregarded these and took Owen straight to the place where he had first seen the body.

Owen walked back with him to the Tree.

'It's a long way to drag someone.'

The tracker shrugged.

'Perhaps he didn't have a donkey,' he said.

It was a long way. You wouldn't have done it lightly. It must have been done deliberately, to make, as Mahmoud had suggested, a point.

But then, it *was* a long way and if it had been done deliberately, premeditated, why had not the attacker thought of the carrying? Here, in the heat, almost every little thing was carried on the back of a donkey. True, the attack had been at night, when it had been cool. All the same, it was a long way.

He said this to Mahmoud.

'Yes,' said Mahmoud, 'I've been thinking that too.'

'Why not a donkey?'

'Because there are other donkeys about. It might have called out.'

'We're some way from the village,' Owen objected.

'Yes, but there are donkeys about. There's one over there, for instance, among those trees by the well.'

Owen nodded, accepting.

'It *had* to be a long way,' said Mahmoud. 'The railway track was where he wanted the body to be in the end. But Ibrahim wasn't going to walk there himself. If he was going to be trapped by a meeting, the meeting would have to be close to the village. Close, but not too close. Here, by the Tree,' said Mahmoud, looking around him, 'would be just about right.'

∽

The Copt had been watching the goings-on with interest. Owen walked over to him.

'Are you here all the time, Daniel?'

'Certainly,' said the Copt. 'It's my property, isn't it?'

'Nights, too?'

'Well, no. I have a wife to keep warm.'

'And where do you keep her warm, Daniel?'

'At Tel-el-Hasan.'

'Ah, Heliopolis? Where they are building?'

'Where they are building, unfortunately. I offered them my land but the Khedive got there first.'

'It's his land, is it?'

'Most of it is just desert. But he claimed that it belongs to him.'

'And you go back there every night?'

'I do.'

'Do you walk?'

'Walk?' said Daniel, astonished. 'Walking is for fellahin. I have a donkey.'

'And at what time is it that you set out from here?'

'When the sun is two fists above the horizon. Leave it any later and it would be dark when I got home. I wouldn't want that. There are bad men about,' he said, looking at the spot where the trackers were crouching. 'Muslims,' he added.

'And when do you return?'

'At sunrise. Leave it any later and who knows how many may have been carving at the Tree.'

'And on the night the man was killed you saw nothing untoward as you left?'

'No.'

'Nor as you came the next morning?'

'What might I have seen?'

'I was just wondering.'

'The other men have already asked me this,' said Daniel. 'Both that one'—pointing at Mahmoud—'and the other one before.'

Owen, following the point, saw again the donkey among the trees.

'That donkey over there: is it yours?'

'It is; and the trees should be mine by rights also. For when the Virgin rested beneath the Tree, she went down to the well for water with which to wash the Child's garments. And when she threw away the water afterwards, trees of holy balsam sprang up. Those trees. Worth a lot of money. And by rights,' said Daniel bitterly, 'they should be mine. For they would not have been there had not the Virgin rested under my Tree.'

'Who do they belong to?'

'There are those in the village who say they are wild trees, that they belong to everyone. But the well isn't wild, is it? Someone put it there. The same with the trees. Someone planted them. And that someone was the Virgin after she had rested under my Tree. They don't belong to everyone; they belong to me.

And that old bastard over there is letting his goats devour my substance!'

The goats were rising on to their hind legs and tearing at the branches. From where they tore, a strong, sweet, herby smell drifted across to Owen.

'Fine beasts!' he said to the old man.

'Two are milking,' said the old man.

'This is a handy place for you,' said Owen. 'Both water and food.'

'They don't like the leaves all that much,' said the old man. 'We might move on soon.'

'You've been here a day or two?'

The old man nodded.

'What do you do at night? Leave them?'

'I stay with them,' said the old man. 'They're used to me.'

'So you were here the other night, the night the man was found?'

He nodded again.

'And did you hear anything that night?'

'I heard the doves in the trees.'

'And then, when it grew dark and the doves settled down, did you hear anything then?'

'The goats were restless.'

'They were disturbed, perhaps?'

'Perhaps,' agreed the old man.

'What by?'

The old man considered.

'People,' he said at last.

'Up here? By the Tree?'

'That's where they were.'

'There were more than one of them, then?'

'That is so.'

'And what did you hear?'

'Talking.'

'Loud talking?'

'Not very loud.'

'Were they fierce with one another?'

'No,' said the old man, surprised. He considered for a moment. 'One of them was a woman,' he volunteered hesitantly.

'Ah? You heard her talking? And the other was a man? Or perhaps there was more than one man?'

'Just the one.'

Owen tried, unsuccessfully, to get more out of him, then went and told Mahmoud.

'She was wrong, then,' said Owen.

'She?'

'Jalila. The woman he had been seeing.'

He told Mahmoud what she had said to Asif.

'She reckoned it would be no good him seeing another woman after what he had been doing with her! Evidently she was wrong.'

'Or lying.'

'I don't think she was lying,' said Owen.

'Probably not. Let us accept, then, that she was wrong. He *was* going out to see another woman.'

'We can't be absolutely sure. But it seems very likely.'

'It would have to have been,' said Mahmoud, thinking, 'a woman in the village. In that case someone else in the village will almost certainly know her.'

❧

'Women in this village are a loose lot!' said Sheikh Isa fiercely.

They had run into him on their way back to Matariya.

'Well, that's the way of it!' said Owen, shaking his head sadly.

'Is it that they do not listen to their husbands' words?' asked Mahmoud sympathetically. 'Or is it that the husbands do not hear *your* words?'

'Women are immoral; men are weak,' said Sheikh Isa.

'Temptresses, all of them!' said Owen.

'That slut Jalila! She should be stoned, for a start!'

'One bad date infects the others,' said Mahmoud.

'They ought to make an example of her! I've been saying that for a long time. But will they listen to me?'

'I expect that's because too many have been seeing her themselves,' said Owen naughtily.

Sheikh Isa glared at him.

'If they have,' he said fiercely, 'then they should mend their ways!'

'Perhaps the fate of Ibrahim will be a lesson to them.'

Sheikh Isa gave him a quick look. He was, for all his vehemence, Owen realized, no fool.

'Was that it?' he said.

'We do not know,' said Mahmoud, 'but we wonder. And we wonder especially who was the other woman that he was seeing.'

'Another?' Sheikh Isa smote his brow. 'Another woman, you say? Besides Jalila?' Mahmoud nodded.

'Whores!' shouted Sheikh Isa. 'All of them! Whores!'

Passers-by in the street looked up with interest.

'Well, possibly not all of them,' said Owen. 'Perhaps, in fact, just one. Apart from Jalila, of course.'

'A woman was speaking with Ibrahim on the night he was killed,' said Mahmoud. 'After he had been to Jalila's. We would like to know who she was.'

'It may be, indeed, it is quite likely, that he had seen her before,' said Owen.

'In which case,' said Mahmoud, 'someone in the village may know her.' Sheikh Isa looked at him thoughtfully.

'They may indeed,' he said. 'There are people in the village who make it their business to know everyone else's business. And tell it!' he shouted suddenly. 'Gossips, slanderers, spies! Women!'

'Well—'

'Come with me!' shouted Sheikh Isa. 'I know who will know!'

❦

An old woman came to the door.

'Tell us!' shouted Sheikh Isa. 'Tell us!'

'Tell you what?'

'Who he was with. Come on! Out with it! Let's have the name of the whore!'

'Which whore?' asked the old woman. 'There are plenty of them.'

'The one who was with Ibrahim that night!'

'You know who was with him that night.'

'Not Jalila, you fool. The other one!'

The woman regarded him unabashed.

'Oh ho!' she said. 'You're waking up, are you?'

'My eyes have been opened!'

'Well, about time, too. But I can't help you.'

'Don't you know?'

'Not for certain. But I could have a pretty good guess.'

'Well then?'

'Oh, no. I couldn't tell you.'

'Why not?' thundered the sheikh.

'You told me not to gossip.'

'This isn't gossip!'

'What is it, then?'

'Why, it's—it's simply giving information. That's all.'

'But that's what I was doing last week when you told me not to!'

'Don't trifle with me, bitch!'

'Oh, no, I couldn't tell you, I'm afraid,' said the old woman, greatly enjoying herself. 'I do know, as a matter of fact, or, at least, I could make a pretty good guess. But I couldn't tell you. It wouldn't be right.'

'Just tell me, you old bitch!'

'My sheikh told me not to!'

Sheikh Isa raised his stick and the old woman darted back behind the door.

'Shame on you!' she said. 'First you tempt me into vice; then you beat me! I shall go to your prayer meeting tomorrow and I shall call out to all the people: "Sheikh Isa tempted me to vice and then when I wouldn't succumb, he threatened to beat me!"'

The stick smashed against the door. Evidently Sheikh Isa was not feared as greatly in the village as Owen had supposed.

Mahmoud decided to intervene.

'You joke, Mother,' he said sternly, 'but this is no laughing matter. A man has died.' The woman opened the door and looked at him.

'Are you the kadi?' she asked.

'I am as the kadi.'

'You've been a long time coming. Justice doesn't get to this place often.'

'It has come now. And it seeks your help. When Ibrahim went out that night, after he had left Jalila, he went out to meet another woman. Do you know who she might have been?'

The old woman looked at him for a moment or two without replying. Then she sighed and said:

'Ibrahim was a fool. He never could leave the women alone. But it's not right that he should die because of that. That's not justice, is it? So I will tell you. I don't know who he went out to see that night. But I know who he had an eye for: Khadija.'

'Khadija?' shouted the sheikh. 'Khadija?'

'That's right.'

'You old bitch! You're just mischief-making!'

'Who is Khadija?' asked Mahmoud.

The woman turned to him.

'Leila's sister.'

'The murdered man's wife,' said Owen.

'You lie, woman!' shouted the sheikh.

'I don't lie!' said the woman defiantly. 'It's true! He's always had an eye for her. Some say he wanted to marry her and not the other one. I don't know about that but I do know he's always had an eye for her, even after he got married.'

'Did you talk to the wife's family?' Owen asked Mahmoud quietly.

'I did. But I didn't talk to her.'

'It is possible,' Sheikh Isa grudgingly acknowledged. 'Though unseemly!' He glared at the old woman.

'Of course, she doesn't come from our village,' said the old woman cunningly.

'That's true!' said Sheikh Isa, struck.

'Where does she come from?' asked Owen.

'Tel-el-Hasan.'

'I must go there,' said Sheikh Isa, 'and tell Sheikh Riyad. Together we will denounce her!'

'Hold back a little,' said Mahmoud. 'We do not know yet that she was the one.'

'He had an eye for her; we know that, don't we?'

'Yes, but we don't know that she had an eye for him.'

'He wouldn't have looked in her direction if she hadn't lured him, would he? Whores! Whores! They're all whores!' shouted Sheikh Isa, as he hurried away.

⟨ತಿಚಿ⟩

Tel-el-Hasan, where the wife's family came from, was a village less than two miles away. Like Matariya, it was a cluster of trees. Although the villages were some four or five miles away from the Nile, they were connected to it by irrigation channels. Their chief course of water, however, was the main Khalig Canal, which became the Ismailiya Canal just beyond Matariya. Again, they were not directly on the canal but connected to it through the irrigation system, a mass of small channels, ditches and furrows which ran water across the fields. There was, though, probably at both Matariya and Tel-el-Hasan, an underground supply of water which the wells were tapping and which accounted for the dense foliage of the trees.

In one of the *gadwals*, or ditches, two small boys were fighting. Mahmoud, for justice even among small boys, stepped down into the ditch and pulled them apart.

'He's smaller than you,' he remonstrated.

'It's a blood feud,' said the bigger boy.

'Shame on you! In the same village?'

'He's not really of this village,' said the bigger boy.

'Yes, I am,' said the smaller boy tearfully.

'No, you're not. That's his house over there!'

He pointed to a small house on the outskirts or, if you were pedantic, just beyond the outskirts of the village.

'That counts as village,' said Mahmoud firmly, and let the boys scamper off.

'Even that little distance!' He shook his head sadly. 'It makes two miles away seem like a foreign country.'

'They marry between villages, though,' said Owen.

'They have to. The trouble is, it doesn't diminish the distance.'

'Was the family bent on feud?'

'They wouldn't say. They wouldn't say anything.'

'You know, this could be solved. It doesn't have to turn into a blood feud. From the point of view of the woman's family, no blood has been shed.'

'From the point of view of the man's family it has, though. If they think it was one of the wife's family, they'll want revenge.'

'Why should it be one of the wife's family?'

'Honour.'

'Do they care about the woman that much?'

'No. But they do care about the family and they say the family's been slighted.'

'Ibrahim's family could pay recompense.'

'Recompense is the last thing it's thinking of at the moment. One of its men has been killed and it wants revenge.'

'It could pay a little and send the wife back.'

'That would make it worse. The wife's family would say it showed a lack of respect. Funnily enough, I think Ibrahim's family would take that view too. They've got no thought of sending her back. They don't like her particularly, all she's had are two daughters, it's just an extra burden on them—and yet it hasn't entered their heads to send her back. She became part of the family by marriage and now it's their job to look after her.

No, what they're really interested in is the man. A man's been killed, their man, and that must be paid for.'

Owen nodded. When he had first come to Egypt he had spent a few months patrolling the desert and knew about feuds and the tribal code of honour.

'The danger is,' he said, 'that they'll kill someone in the wife's family, and then there'll be another death to be paid for, and so it'll go on.'

'These villagers!' said Mahmoud.

'Let's hope it's not someone in the wife's family.'

'Let's hope we find out who it is,' said Mahmoud, 'before they do.'

The roof of the house was piled high with brushwood, vegetables and buffalo dung, all in close proximity to each other. From the corners of the roof, strings of onions dangled down, each onion as vast as a melon. Poor the people might be, hungry they were not. Where there was such food there must be men to earn it or grow it, and, sure enough, inside the house there were three of them.

'You again?' said the older brother unwelcomingly to Mahmoud.

'It is justice for your sister that I seek,' said Mahmoud softly.

'We will look after that.'

'No,' said Mahmoud, shaking his head. 'You will not.'

The brother stared at him for a moment and then looked at Owen.

'Who is he?'

'The Mamur Zapt.'

The man flinched slightly. Old memories, the old legend, died hard.

'What is it you want?'

'To talk to Khadija.'

'Khadija! There is no point. Talk to us.'

'I talked to you the other day,' said Mahmoud. 'Now I would talk with Khadija.'

The men looked at each other.

'She is not here,' said one of the other brothers defiantly.

'Then I will wait until she returns,' said Mahmoud, settling himself comfortably.

'You cannot speak with her!'

'Why is it important that I do not speak with her?'

'It is not important; she is a woman, that is all.'

'Would you like my friend to go into the women's quarters and fetch her out? He has the right.'

It was true. The Mamur Zapt had right of entry into all houses in Cairo, including harems. Whether that right extended as far out as Tel-el-Hasan, however, was questionable.

It was also questionable how far the right could be made to stick. Only two years before, not far from here, a policeman had been shot while conducting his investigations.

Owen stirred, as if ready to get to his feet. The men looked at each other.

A woman came through the door which led to the inner room.

'Let them talk to me,' she said.

'Khadija?'

She nodded.

'I will do the talking,' said the eldest brother.

The woman stood with arms folded. She was not exactly veiled, but had pulled her headdress across her face so that they could not see it.

'Did you know Ibrahim?' asked Mahmoud, putting his question, however, not to her but to her brother, as was the convention.

'How could she?' said the brother.

'I am asking her.'

'I knew my sister's husband,' she said quietly.

'She knew him as a sister-in-law should.'

'I have no doubt about that. But was it the same with him? Would he have known her, that is, would he have liked to have known her, in a different way?'

'You'll have to ask him,' said one of the other brothers, and laughed.

'That is a disrespectful question,' said the oldest brother.

'It has to be asked. For others are asking it too.'

'They are?'

The oldest brother's cheeks tautened.

'That village makes a jest of us, brother,' said one of the others angrily.

Mahmoud held up his hand.

'Not a jest. And they show no disrespect. For all they say is that he behaved disrespectfully to you.'

'In disrespecting us,' said the woman angrily, 'he disrespected my sister.'

'It was, however, by eye alone?'

'He would have liked it otherwise.'

'But it was by eye alone?'

'With me, it was. But not with my sister. With her it was by deed.'

'He shamed her publicly,' growled one of the brothers.

'By going to Jalila?'

'Every night. He made no secret of it. And nor did she. "I can give you sons," she said, "even if your wife can't."'

'Who was she to talk?' said the woman fiercely. 'How many sons had she? At least Leila had had daughters. And sons would have come. They always do in our family. Look at them!'

She pointed to her brothers.

'I am puzzled,' said Owen. 'First, he left your sister for Jalila. And then he would have left Jalila for you?'

'If he had had the chance!' said Khadija.

'He wouldn't have got the chance,' said one of the brothers angrily. 'What do you think we are: men who make their sisters into whores?'

'Whores!' shouted a familiar voice in the street.

Owen and Mahmoud looked at each other.

'Oh God!' said Owen. 'It's Sheikh Isa!'

⊙⫘⊙

Out in the street was Sheikh Isa, together with another religious sheikh, as old, venerable and, probably, as irascible as himself, supported by an interested crowd of onlookers.

'This is untimely!' said Owen.

'God's work does not wait on man's convenience,' said Sheikh Isa unyieldingly.

'God's work? You call it God's work to come to a house and denounce a woman who may well be guiltless?'

'Innocence is for God to judge, not man!' bellowed the sheikh. 'Man looks only at incidentals but God sees into the very heart!'

'There's nothing wrong with my heart!' said Khadija stoutly.

'There'll be something wrong with yours in a minute!' said one of the brothers, diving back into the house.

Mahmoud caught him as he re-emerged carrying a rifle.

'Enough!' shouted Owen.

He forced the gun out of the man's hands and covered the other two.

'Stay where you are!'

'To the *caracol* with them!' shouted Sheikh Isa, enraged.

Mahmoud looked at Owen.

'That might not be such a bad idea.'

Owen nodded.

'Fetch me rope!' he commanded.

Some men ran into a nearby house and returned with a coil.

'I'm arresting you,' said Mahmoud to the brother he was holding. He tied the man's hands.

'And you! And you!' he said to the other brothers.

'We haven't done anything!' shouted the brothers.

'Let's keep it like that. Turn round!'

'What about me?' cried Khadija.

'Whore!' shouted Sheikh Isa. 'You're the one who started it all!'

One of the brothers made a grab for the gun. Owen brought it down on his arm. Mahmoud caught him from behind and tied his hands deftly.

'You stay out of this!' Owen said to Sheikh Isa. 'You stay here!' he said to Khadija.

'And you,' he said to the other sheikh, 'see that she comes to no harm!'

Mahmoud finished tying the brothers and stepped back.

'Why are you doing this to them?' demanded Khadija.

'To save them from being shot,' said Owen in an aside.

Chapter 5

The station at Matariya did not amount to much. It was merely a stop in the desert. There was no platform and no building, apart from a water tower. There was normally, however, a ticket collector, who sat on a chair under a solitary acacia tree and took tickets when they were offered.

This morning, though, when Owen climbed down from the train, he was not there. The chair stood in its usual place, unoccupied. Owen, who had been under the impression that the collector was permanently fixed to it, was a little surprised; surprised, too, that at this halt, when normally the only things moving were the little desert sparrows that liked to assemble on the arm that swung out from the water tower, there were people scurrying about.

When the train pulled out he saw what it was all about. On the other side of the track, about a hundred yards away, was a large ostrich pen and this morning it was the scene of considerable commotion. Great birds were running agitatedly about the pen, flapping their huge wings as if attempting to take off. They ran manically, not heeding where they were going, and from time to time one bore down on the fence near the station. Whenever that happened, men working on the fence would rush out and wave their arms and shout and at the last moment the huge bird, about nine feet high and twenty stones in weight, would panic and swerve and head off again across the desert.

It was all very exciting and Owen could see at once why it had attracted a crowd of onlookers, including the ticket collector. He could see now, too, that there was a gap in the fence, which the men were working on.

This side of the fence, near the track, a man was lying on the ground and a small group of people were bending over him.

Owen walked across.

The man was holding his neck and groaning.

'Be of good cheer, Ja'affar,' said one of the men bending over him. 'We have sent for the barber.'

'I don't need a barber,' groaned the man on the ground, 'I need a *hakim*.'

'The barber is cheaper, Ja'affar,' advised one of the men.

Ja'affar just groaned.

'Perhaps Zaghlul will send for a *hakim*,' suggested another of the men.

'Zaghlul?' said the man on the ground. 'Not if it costs money! He might send for the sheikh to pray for me.'

'Here is an effendi,' said one of the men. 'Perhaps he is a *hakim*.'

'I am afraid not,' said Owen. 'But let a *hakim* be summoned and I will pay.'

He looked down at the man on the ground.

'Why, it's you!' he said, surprised, recognizing the man he'd spoken to with Asif. 'Of course! You work at the farm.'

'That bloody bird! I didn't see it coming.'

'It got through the fence, Ja'affar, and ran away.'

'Did it? Well, old man Zaghlul will be more worried about that than about me!'

'Owen! Owen! Is that you?' called a voice.

Owen looked up. There, surprisingly, was Malik, the Pasha's son; and there, even more surprisingly, for such things had only just come to Egypt, was a shining, brand-new motor car.

'Come on! Get in!'

Owen walked over.

'A bird has got out! We'll have a hunt!'

'Well, I don't know—'

'Come on, man. Get in!'

'There's a man who's been hurt—'

'A broken collarbone! Nothing!'

Malik took him by the arm and almost dragged him in.

'Remember! I'll pay for the *hakim*,' Owen called over his shoulder.

'You don't need to do that, old boy,' said Malik. 'These fellows are pretty hardy. A few days' rest will put him right. He'll be back to work in no time.'

'The air here is very good,' said one of the other men in the car. 'Very healthy.'

There were two other men in the car—Egyptians, and very rich. There was also a remarkable array of guns.

'Grabbed all I had,' said Malik. 'I don't know which one will be best for the job. Never shot an ostrich before.'

'Do we have to shoot it?'

'Oh yes. Why not?'

'Well, it's…wouldn't you call it farm stock?'

'I'd call it game. Or wild fowl. Yes, wild fowl, I think. That would suggest a fowling piece. We have a fowling piece, don't we, Ahmed? Or perhaps that's too light. It's a big bird, after all. Yes, definitely too light. One of the others, then.'

The car bounced over the desert.

'It's the only way,' said Malik.

'Only way?'

'To hunt. Tried it on horse but you never get close enough. Not with gazelles, you don't. An ostrich would be about the same, don't you think? Pretty fast.'

'It's got a small head, Malik,' said one of the other men.

'Have to be the body, then. Even that will be tricky. Moving target, moving gun platform. Damned exciting! Exciting, isn't it, Owen?'

'Oh, yes.'

'Glad I spotted you. We'll go into the Racing Club afterwards for a bit of lunch. They ought to stand us lunch, you know. After shooting an ostrich. Doing them a favour.'

'Doing them a favour?'

'Yes. The damned birds are always getting out and attacking the racehorses.'

'I don't think they actually *attack* them, Malik. It's just that they scare them.'

'Same thing, isn't it? They're a damned nuisance. Someone ought to speak to that old fool, Zaghlul.'

'We do. Often.'

'That farm is a liability.'

'Oh, I don't know, Malik,' objected one of the others. 'It's very picturesque, don't you think? Interesting for the tourists.'

'Well, make it more interesting,' said Malik. 'Turn it into a game reserve. Sell shooting rights. God, that's an idea! I say, I'm quite a businessman, aren't I? What an idea! Let's put it to the Syndicate.'

'Old man Zaghlul will never agree.'

'Buy him out. I'll get the Syndicate to buy him out.'

'I think it's tried, Malik. It would like the land. But Zaghlul will have none of it.'

'We'll have to make him see reason, then.'

Over on the horizon, Owen suddenly saw a group of horsemen.

'Over there! Over there!' shouted Ahmed excitedly.

Malik pointed the car towards them and sounded his horn.

'Tally ho!' shouted Ahmed. He looked at Owen. 'That's what they shout in England, don't they?'

'I imagine so.'

They didn't go in for hunts much in the part of Wales that he came from.

The car bumped crazily across the desert, threatening at every moment to throw them out.

'Damned exciting, isn't it?' said Malik, teeth gleaming.

They came up with the horsemen. An old man in ragged Bedouin dress and with a rifle slung on his back rode over to them and gesticulated angrily.

Malik took no notice.

'By God, there it is!' he shouted.

For out in the desert in front of them a solitary ostrich wheeled and scudded.

'Tally ho!' cried Malik, leading the car in its direction.

The horsemen scattered. Owen just had time to see the old Bedouin unslinging his gun and then he had to cling on for dear life.

'Load the gun, Ahmed!' shouted Malik.

'Which one?'

'Any one!'

The ostrich, startled, ran before them.

'You're gaining, Malik!'

'Got the gun?'

But just at that moment the front wheels of the car ran into a deep drift. They all pitched forward. Owen suddenly found himself sprawling across the bonnet.

'Give me the gun!' shouted Malik.

Owen hauled himself back.

There was a loud explosion.

Ahead, the ostrich checked, veered and then ran off at right angles.

'Try another one, Malik!'

But the distance was now too great. Malik, disgustedly, climbed out of the car. Across the desert Owen saw groups of horsemen converging on the ostrich.

It took them nearly an hour to dig themselves out of the drift and to get going again. The car bumped across to where, now, the horsemen seemed to have the ostrich secured.

It was lying on the ground trapped in a huge net. The men had tied its feet together. It lay there, sides heaving. Men were holding its neck. From time to time it reached round and tried to peck at their hands.

Malik sighed.

'Damned difficult shot!' he said. 'It would have been a beauty if I'd brought it off. How about a drink?'

⁂

'Vermin!' said the man at the bar of the Racing Club. 'That's what they are!'

'Heard my idea?' said Malik happily. 'Turn the damned farm into a game reserve. Sell shooting rights. It would be a big attraction.'

'Ostriches and horses don't mix,' said the first man. 'The ostriches frighten the horses and the horses frighten the ostriches. You've got to keep them apart. That farm's too close to the racetrack.'

'It's three miles away!' objected someone.

'That's not far if they're going to break out. And what about the training gallops?'

'They're not going to be breaking out all the time!'

'I should hope not. They're damned dangerous beasts. Break a horse's leg in no time.'

'Dangerous, are they?' said one of the Belgians uneasily. 'We'll have to watch that. An ostrich farm is one thing—in fact, it could be quite attractive, couldn't it? An unusual feature—but if they're dangerous, it's quite another.'

'Could you pay the old man to put them down?'

'How many are there?'

'Several hundred.'

'Cost too much. And he might not be willing.'

'My idea's better,' said Malik. 'Get people to pay to put them down.'

'I say, Malik, there's a woman!'

They all scurried across to the window.

'It's Salah-el-Din's girl.'

'A bit bold, isn't she?'

'I'm going over,' said Malik, making for the door. 'You coming?' he said over his shoulder to Owen.

'I don't think so. In fact'—he glanced at his watch—'I ought to be making a move.'

'Don't go yet,' said one of the Belgians. 'We'd like to have a word with you.'

They led him away into a corner of the barroom and ordered more drinks. From where he was sitting he could see out through the window. Beside the racetrack was a strip of newly planted grass and on it a girl was walking. A servant held a parasol over her head.

'A little forward, yes?' said one of the Belgians.

'All right on the boulevards,' said Raoul, the one he'd played tennis with. 'But here?'

'She's very young,' said Owen.

'Their tastes are different here.'

As he watched, he saw Salah-el-Din come up and join her and then, a moment after, Malik at the run.

'An ambitious man, Salah,' said one of the Belgians. 'He has big plans.'

'It's not always a good idea for a district mamur to have big plans,' said Owen.

'No. And you yourself: do you have big plans?'

'It's not always a good idea for British officials to have big plans, either.'

'Not in the sense you mean, no. But you must make plans of some sort. You have to retire so early. Then what?'

'Good question,' said Owen.

'Unless your government is very different from ours, the pension is piffling.'

'I'm some way off drawing a pension yet,' said Owen.

'That's the time to make plans.'

Owen, used to such approaches, was not bothered. The conversation turned to other things. The Belgians said the project was going quite well. Building, with plenty of space and cheap labour, was no problem. The only difficulty, if there was one, was in matching development to cash-income flow.

'Any building project is a long-term one,' said Raoul. 'The trouble is, if it's too long-term, the people financing it start getting bothered. So what you try to do is get something going quite early on that yields a cash flow.'

'Like a gambling house?' said Owen.

Raoul laughed.

'It would help. But the hotel's the main thing. Once you start attracting people in, they'll start spending money.'

'Building houses and selling them isn't enough?'

'It's all right. In the long run. But in the short run we want more spend. That's why the racetrack is important. If it's attractive enough, people will come here even if they don't live here.'

'Provided they can get here.'

'Yes,' said Raoul, 'that's the key. Roads, rail, even trams. We intend to get the tramway system extended out to here.'

'Out to here?' said Owen incredulously. 'That'll be the day!'

'You see space,' said Raoul. 'We see buildings.'

'What a horrifying thought!'

'It's the future,' said Raoul.

Down below, Amina came to the end of her perambulating and set off in the direction of home, accompanied by her father, and Malik.

'And meanwhile,' said Owen, 'until the houses get built and the tramway system is extended, how are you getting on with the new railway?'

'It's coming along,' said Raoul. He frowned. 'But too slowly.'

'You need it for the cash flow?'

'We need it for the cash flow. Now that the racecourse has been built, we can't afford not to have it coming. We were thinking,' he said, looking at Owen, 'of getting the men to work on Fridays.'

'Fridays! But that's the Muslim Sabbath!'

'We work on Sundays already, you know.'

'Yes, but that's different. This is a Muslim country.'

'How religious is Egypt?'

'When it comes to working on the Sabbath, you'll find it's pretty religious,' said Owen.

౼

'Blasphemy! Sacrilege! Desecration!' shouted Sheikh Isa.

There was a larger crowd around the tabernacle than usual, including this time a number of younger men, some of whom Owen thought he remembered from the railway.

'Ordinarily I wouldn't agree with him,' said Ja'affar, 'but this time I think he's got a point.'

'It's all right for you, Ja'affar,' said one of the men whom Owen thought he remembered from the railway—Abdul was his name? 'It doesn't apply to those working at the ostrich farm.'

'Yet,' said one of the other labourers.

Ja'affar, shocked, turned on him.

'You don't think old man Zaghlul—?'

'He's a mean old skinflint. Doesn't miss a trick. If they get away with it on the railway, he'll start asking why he can't introduce it on the farm.'

'You're all right for the moment anyway, Ja'affar,' said the barber. 'You can't work with that arm.'

They were sitting on the ground just beyond the outer ring of Sheikh Isa's listeners, far enough away to demonstrate their independence, yet close enough to hear what was being said. The barber had temporarily moved his shop there; that is, his chair, his bowls and his implements.

And also his cronies. This was a different congregation from Sheikh Isa's: younger, more dissident, free-thinking. It included, besides the wounded Ja'affar, several of the men who worked on the railway, among them the man who had acted as their spokesman in the confrontation over the removal of Ibrahim's body. It also included the dead man's brother.

'You're right,' said the man who had acted as spokesman. Wahid appeared to be his name. 'Ordinarily I wouldn't agree with the old sheikh either. But he's got a point. If this working-on-the-Sabbath idea goes ahead, soon they'll have us all working on the Sabbath. You, Ja'affar, me, Ismail—not you, though,' he said, looking at Owen.

Owen had come there to pay his dues. It had turned out, however, that a *hakim* had not in the end been sent for.

'He would have had to have come all the way from the city, Effendi,' explained the barber. 'Besides, to what end? What is a broken collarbone? I can fix that.'

'You said it didn't need fixing,' said Ja'affar accusingly. 'You said it would get better of its own accord.'

'And so it will. The sling is there just to support the arm so that it will not put weight on it. And to show old man Zaghlul that there really is something wrong with you.'

Ja'affar had seemed not just satisfied but mending, so Owen had contented himself with settling the barber's bill, an action which had endeared him both to Ja'affar and to the barber and his ring of cronies.

'I work all the time,' said Owen, smiling. .

He had accepted a cup of tea and sat down in the circle with the others; from where he could, conveniently, hear what Sheikh Isa said and at the same time sample local opinion. One thing the issue of Friday-working did appear to have done was to have pushed Ibrahim's death out of the forefront of men's minds. If it had, that would help Mahmoud. It would give him more time in which to track down Ibrahim's killer and prevent the whole thing from turning into a revenge feud. If, of course, the killing was purely a local matter.

But now what was this? Sheikh Isa was connecting the two things.

'How many more signs does God have to send? First, the Tree; then poor, murdered Ibrahim! Are not the signs there to be read? And is there a man so stupid that he cannot read them? Lust, adultery and death everywhere; discord and disharmony. God piles sign upon sign. Nature revolts. Yesterday, but yesterday, here, yes, here in this very village, an ostrich breaks out and savages a man! What is this but God's way of showing us that we have gone too far, that if we transgress the bounds of order, so too with Nature! Stop now! Turn back this foolish thing, this monster, this sacrilegious beast! Stop this railway now!'

Wahid, the labourers' spokesman, stood up and applauded vigorously.

☙

Owen suddenly had trouble at home. It began auspiciously enough with an invitation to dinner from Zeinab's father, Nuri Pasha. When he arrived, Zeinab, who was coming independently, had not yet got there so Owen took off his shoes and climbed up on the *liwan* beside Nuri for a good chat. The *liwan* was a dais at one end of the *mandar'ah*, or reception room, where the host would lie, on large *divans*, or cushions, and, if his guests were sufficiently favoured, invite them to recline also.

Nuri was a traditionalist when it came to comforts and beside the *liwan* was a stand on which he kept his coffee-sets, water-pipes and dishes of Turkish delight and nougat. His comforts extended more widely, too, and on the floor above was a harem-room well stocked with wives and concubines. Nuri, however, was growing older and no longer found the performance of the concubines as satisfactory as he had once done, something which he attributed to the declining standards of the age.

He had never, in any case, found anyone to match Zeinab's mother, who had once been the most famous courtesan in Cairo. Nuri had loved her dearly and recklessly, proposing marriage to her on a number of occasions. His conduct had been for several years the scandal and glee of Cairo society. Zeinab's mother, as independent as her daughter, had tactfully refused his proposals, unwilling, she said, to accept the sacrifice of standing and career that such a step would mean for the man she loved. Career, replied Nuri—he had been young then—was transitory; love was permanent. And, indeed, their relationship had lasted for quite a time; until, in fact, Zeinab's mother died, leaving behind her something less transitory in the shape of Zeinab.

Nuri, a Francophile and, in those days, a modernizer, had decided to bring up his daughter in the Western manner, want-ing her to grow up to be as spirited and free-thinking as her mother. Now, having done so, he was not quite so sure that it had been a good idea.

What, for example, about marriage? A match with a wealthy Pasha or Pasha's son was the obvious thing, but Pashas and sons alike were frankly terrified of her. Besides, the years were going by and she was now twenty-eight. Girls got married at half her age.

Zeinab herself was beginning to be uncomfortably aware of this. Owen, fortunately, was not, and for the time being she intended to make the most of a relationship with someone who thought she was normal.

Nuri poured out these and other woes to Owen as they lay on the *liwan*, and Owen replied, as he always did, that Zeinab would make up her own mind about these things and that nothing either he or Nuri did would alter this in the slightest.

They were in full, contented flow when Zeinab arrived, brandishing a large gilt-edged card.

'What is this?' she demanded.

Nuri took it gingerly.

'It is an invitation to a reception to mark the formal opening of the Racing Club at Heliopolis,' he replied.

'What have I to do with Racing Clubs, what have I to do with jumped-up, parvenu places like Heliopolis?' she demanded. 'What, more to the point,' she said, looking fiercely at Owen, 'have you to do with them?'

'Nothing,' said Owen. 'I'm just going to the reception, that's all.'

'It's that girl,' said Zeinab.

'What girl?' said Owen, bewildered.

'That one I saw you with the other day. In Anton's.'

'Salah-el-Din's daughter? She's just a child.'

'I know what she is,' said Zeinab, 'and it certainly isn't a child!'

'Who's Salah-el-Din?' asked Nuri, interested.

'The new mamur at Heliopolis.'

'And he shops at Anton's?'

Nuri looked thoughtful.

'It's odd that you should have been invited,' said Owen, puzzled. Egyptian women, even if they were Pasha's daughters, were hardly ever invited to public events.

Zeinab, however, was in a mood to take umbrage.

'You don't want me to be there, is that it?' she demanded, switching tack.

'Of course not. I'm just puzzled, that's all. You've never had anything to do with racing. How did they come to pick on you?'

He took the card from Nuri. The names of the Club's new committee were printed at the bottom.

'Malik?' he said. 'Do you think it could be Malik?'

'That man I told Anton to throw out?'

'Malik?' said Nuri. 'Which Malik?'

'Abd-al-Jamal's son,' said Owen.

'You told Anton to throw him out?'

'Certainly.'

'Oh, my God!' said Nuri.

'He's a gross pig.'

'Yes, but Abd-al-Jamal's son!'

'What difference does that make?'

'Abd-al-Jamal's very powerful. And very rich. Besides—'

'Yes?'

'I've been talking to him recently,' said Nuri unhappily.

'So?'

'Well—'

'What,' said Zeinab in sudden fury, 'have you been talking to him about?'

'Well—'

'If,' said Zeinab ominously, 'you have been talking to him about marriage—'

'No, no, no!' said Nuri hastily. 'Only in general.'

'Because if it gets particular—'

'No question of that. No question at all…he is, of course, very rich.'

Owen could see it all too clearly. Nuri's finances were permanently straitened; and what better way of relieving them than marrying off his daughter to the son of one of the wealthiest Pashas in Egypt?

'No!' shouted Zeinab, stamping her foot. 'I won't!'

'There's absolutely no question—'

'I would kill myself first!'

'No question—'

'No, I wouldn't,' said Zeinab, suddenly stopping.

'You wouldn't?' said Nuri, heart beginning to lift.

'No. I would kill him. In fact,' said Zeinab magnificently, 'I will go and kill him now!'

And swept out.

⁂

Nuri and Owen sat for a moment in stunned silence.

'You don't think—?' said Nuri hesitantly.

'Not immediately,' said Owen.

'She is a resolute girl.'

'It takes a bit of time.'

'Abd-al-Jamal's an old friend of mine. I would hate—'

'I'll talk to her. I'll suggest she waits until the contingency arises.'

'It was only in passing. We were really talking about my investment.'

'What investment is this?'

'In the Heliopolis Oasis Scheme.'

'I thought you hadn't any money?'

'I'm hoping this will give me some.'

They wouldn't give him some for nothing, thought Owen. Nuri was too astute not to know this. So what was he giving them? Zeinab? But surely he must have known what her reaction would be? Even if he hadn't known that she had already taken a dislike to Malik.

But Zeinab herself had been behaving a little oddly lately. What was she going on about that girl for? If the kid had been a bit older he could have understood it. But she was just a child! He couldn't make it out at all.

But what he could make out was that someone was trying to involve Nuri in the Heliopolis Scheme. What were they after? Was it Zeinab? Who had the suggestion about the marriage come from? Nuri—or Malik? Did Malik have his eye on Zeinab? He thought it not impossible.

But the attempt to involve Nuri must have emanated from the Syndicate, not Malik, and they surely would not be interested in Zeinab. They would be after something else. And it would not be Nuri, not in himself. Pasha though he was and useful though his name might be on the prospectus, there were Pashas in plenty who would be as good and whose names were already there. No, it was something, or someone, else that they were after. And Owen was beginning to have a feeling that it might be him.

Chapter 6

There had been a sharp wind overnight which had blown the sand in from the desert. It lay everywhere; on the slats of the shutters, on the top of Owen's desk in a thin film, in a neat little pile inside his sun helmet hanging on the back of the door. It had got into the filing cabinet and made the papers gritty to touch; it had, despite the cloth folded lovingly by his orderly over the top of the water jug, got into the water so that it tasted of sand.

Everyone was out of sorts. In the orderly office the bearers were unusually subdued. Cleaners were going around ineffectively trying to sweep up the sand. Nikos, the Mamur Zapt's austere Official Clerk, was in a fury, pulling open drawers and inspecting the damage, wondering, madly, whether to have all papers retyped to restore their pristine purity.

McPhee, the Deputy Commandant, normally Boy Scoutish in his cheerfulness, stuck his head in at the door dolefully.

'More to come,' he said, and went off up the corridor.

Yussef, Owen's orderly, who could read Owen's mind but nothing else, padded along the corridor with a fresh pot of coffee. It, too, tasted of sand.

The telephone rang.

'It's the Parquet,' said Nikos, handing Owen the phone.

It was Mahmoud, as Nikos would normally have said. This morning, though, he felt particularly ungiving.

'The courts are closed,' said Mahmoud. 'Sand everywhere. I was thinking of going over to Matariya. Like to come?'

Owen would like to be anywhere but in this grit-tasting office.

'Got to go out,' he said to McPhee as he passed him in the corridor.

'Lucky devil!' said McPhee, bound to his place by duty and, thought Owen, lack of imagination.

He met Mahmoud at the Pont de Limoun. All trains were at a standstill, including those going to Marg, and therefore, Matariya.

'I'll see if they've got a buggy,' said Owen. 'They'll be sending something out to clear the line.'

The booking clerk now regarded him as an old friend.

'But certainly, Effendi! At once! Only it has not come back yet.'

'When will it come back?'

'Ah, well, Effendi…'

'*Bokra?*'

'That's it, Effendi! Tomorrow! Yes, certainly. Tomorrow.'

Mahmoud turned away.

'Hold on!' said Owen. 'This is only the start of the story. Go and check,' he said to the clerk.

The clerk went happily off. It had been a good morning; he had been able to say 'no' to everybody.

'Just tell him it's the Mamur Zapt!' Owen called after him.

A few moments later the clerk came scurrying back.

'Effendi! It's just come in!' he cried joyfully.

'I'm against all this,' muttered Mahmoud wrathfully, as he followed Owen up the platform.

'Privilege?' said Owen. 'It doesn't usually get me very far. But I've met these blokes before.'

'Not privilege,' said Mahmoud, frowning. 'The way these people muck you around!'

Mahmoud lived continually in the hope of a better, brighter Egypt. He worked for it with all his energy; and he couldn't understand why other people didn't do the same.

The buggy was empty apart from tools and water. Owen and Mahmoud settled down and the two-man crew began pumping the vehicle along.

In the cuttings the track had escaped the drift of the sand, but out in the open it had obviously had to be cleared away. Fresh piles of sand lay beside the track.

Out in the desert the wind was still blowing. Puffs of sand raced the buggy along the track, rising up sometimes into a cloud and then dying down again before scudding on at knee-high level.

The crew pulled their headdresses across their faces.

'It's a waste of time clearing all this,' one said. 'It'll soon be back.'

There was plenty of sand on the line already and the buggy slowed appreciably. The piles beside the track grew in size.

Ahead of them they could see men working on the line. The buggy came to a stop just short of them.

'This is as far as we go,' the men said.

The Belgian foreman came towards them.

'Oh, it's you, is it?' he said. 'A fine business this is!' He went up to the buggy and peered in. 'Got the picks?' He moved some of the tools. 'They've sent us more bloody spades!' he said disgustedly. 'Picks!' he said to the buggy men. 'I asked for picks! The sand's packed hard. Go back and tell them. Tell Mustapha: I want picks, picks! I've got to loosen the sand.'

The buggy men shrugged and got back into the buggy. A moment or two later it moved off again, slowly.

'This bloody country!' said the Belgian.

Owen and Mahmoud walked up the line to where the men were working. Great, deep drifts of sand lay across the track. The men were shovelling it aside with wooden spades. It was hard work and the sweat was running down their faces.

'They've been working all morning,' said the foreman. 'You can't expect them to go on all day. They're supposed to be sending me another shift. When I saw the buggy I thought it was them coming. You didn't see any signs, did you?'

'I'm afraid not,' said Owen.

'Well, I'm going to give them a spell in a moment or two,' said the foreman. 'Let them brew up. Water's all very well but you want something with a bit of bite in it, if you're working like this. That's so, isn't it, Abdul?' he said to one of the workmen.

The man straightened up and smiled.

'You want something to take away the taste of the sand,' he said. He resumed shovelling.

'They work hard,' said the Belgian defensively. 'I've never said they didn't.'

He looked out across the desert.

'I was hoping the wind would drop,' he said.

'It doesn't look like it,' said Owen, uncomfortably aware of the particles of sand stinging his face.

'What will you do if it gets up?' asked Mahmoud.

'That's just what I'm wondering,' said the foreman.

A new layer of sand, blown in by the wind, was already covering the track that had previously been cleared.

'We'll have to get them back if it gets any worse,' he said. 'I've got some more men working further up the line. It'll need two trips.' He looked out across the desert. 'Maybe it won't come to that,' he said. 'I hope not. We've got to get this line finished.'

The wind now seemed to be dying down again.

'I've got to go up the line,' said the foreman. He looked at Owen and Mahmoud. 'What were you here for, anyway?'

'We were hoping to go to Matariya.'

The foreman looked dubious.

'I don't know if that's a good idea,' he said. 'Ever been caught in a dust storm?'

'Yes,' said Owen.

'Well, you'll know what I mean.'

'There's more wind out here than there was in the city,' said Mahmoud.

'There's more wind than there was when I came out first thing. If I were you I wouldn't risk it. Catch the next buggy back. You lot,' he called to the workmen, 'can take a spell. Twenty minutes, mind! No longer!'

He marched off. The men put down their spades with alacrity and gathered in the lee of a small dune. Someone brought out a primus stove and put a kettle on it.

Mahmoud looked at Owen.

'He's probably right,' said Owen.

Mahmoud nodded.

'The buggy will be back in a bit,' said the workmen. 'Come over here out of the wind.'

Owen and Mahmoud lay down beside them on the dune. Several of the workmen took out coloured handkerchiefs and unwrapped bread and onions, which they offered hospitably to Owen and Mahmoud. They declined the food but accepted the hot black tea.

'Hard work,' said Mahmoud sympathetically.

'It is that,' said his neighbour.

'The worst thing is,' said one of the other men, 'that we're going to have to do it all again.'

'This wind, you mean?'

'It's not going to amount to anything,' said one of the other workmen, looking at the sky. 'It'll be easy enough to sweep it off the rails.'

'We don't want it too easy,' said someone. 'The longer this job lasts, the better.'

'That's not what the Belgians think!' said someone.

They all laughed.

'It's get-it-all-done-in-a-hurry with them!'

'That's why they want this Friday-working.'

'I don't agree with that. It's not going to make much difference to them, but it makes a lot of difference to us. You don't want back-breaking working *every* day!'

There was a mutter of agreement.

'You want to be able to sleep it off, don't you? I mean, six days a week is all very well, you can cope with that. It doesn't go on forever, after all. But if you're doing it every day without a break, it gets on top of you.'

'There's not much you can do about it, though, is there? It's all very well Wahid saying come out on strike, but where will that get us?'

Owen noticed now that Wahid, their spokesman on the previous occasion he had talked to them, wasn't there.

'You've got to do something!'

'I don't know there's a lot you can do. If you walk out, all they'll do is get somebody else in.'

'They might not be so keen. Not if it's Friday-working.'

'There's plenty who'd jump at the chance. It's only for a month or two, isn't it? And you get extra money.'

'You work extra for it, though, don't you?'

'There are plenty who wouldn't mind that. We've done all the work; why should we give them the money?'

There was a general mutter of agreement.

'You've got to do something, though.'

'Yes, but what?'

'We should get Wahid to speak to them. In everybody's name.'

'A fat lot of good that would do! Where did it get Ibrahim that time?'

'At least he made the point.'

'Yes, but where did it get us? They went on just the same as they'd always done. If you don't like it, they said, you know what you can do.'

'I don't reckon it'd be so easy for them to say that this time. They've got to get the job done quickly. That's what all this is about.'

'They're more likely to get rid of us, then, aren't they?'

'No, they're not. It'd take time to get other men in.'

'Not that much time. About a day, I'd say. And anyway, where would that get us? Out of a job!'

The discussion continued, not very animatedly. On the whole the workmen seemed resigned to the prospect of Friday-working.

'After all,' they said, 'it's only for a few weeks, isn't it?'

The foreman came into view, walking along the track towards them.

The workmen stood up and picked up their spades.

'Where's Wahid, then, this morning?' Owen asked one of them. 'Isn't he with you?'

The men looked around.

'He's up the line, I think.'

'Come on, then!' said the foreman, hurrying up. 'Back to it!'

The men pointed back along the line. The buggy was approaching, crammed full with men.

'It's the next shift,' said the foreman, relieved. 'That's more like it.'

Owen and Mahmoud went back with the buggy. As they left the Pont de Limoun, Owen said:

'Well, a pity. But not altogether wasted.'

'No,' said Mahmoud. 'Definitely not!'

⁂

'If it's that kind of information you're after,' said the Syndicate's voice on the other end of the telephone, 'then the man you want is Salah-el-Din.'

'Salah-el-Din? The mamur of Heliopolis?'

'That's right.'

Owen was surprised. He had been unaware of this side of Salah's activities.

'Would you like to speak to him?'

'Yes. But things are a bit disrupted between here and Heliopolis. The sand—'

'We can put you through if you like.'

Owen was surprised again. So far as he knew the police station at Heliopolis wasn't connected up yet.

'It's his home number.'

'Home number!'

Owen had never met anyone with a home telephone before. Even the Consul-General didn't have one. The Ministries were now connected by phone and so were the banks and some of the biggest companies. It was catching on, no doubt; but telephones at home!

'Well, yes, please. If it's not too much of a problem.'

'No problem at all.'

And in a moment or two he heard Salah's voice on the line.

Yes, he could certainly supply Owen with the information he needed, would be glad to, in fact. Perhaps they could meet?'

'I'd come over,' said Owen, 'but things are a bit disrupted—'

It was better now, Salah assured him. The Syndicate had pulled all stops out in an effort to get communications working again. The roads were virtually clear, he could come up on the buggy if he liked, and the train to Marg, calling at Matariya, was functioning normally.

Perhaps that would be the best bet, if Owen didn't mind taking the trouble. He, Salah, would be glad to come into the Bab-el-Khalk, if Owen would prefer. But he had to go over to Matariya Station anyway this morning, to read the owner of the ostrich farm the riot act, and if Owen wouldn't mind meeting him there—

The sand had, indeed, been removed from the line and the train ran smoothly. The wind had died down and the sky cleared and when Owen got off the train at Matariya he found the air unusually clean and fresh and for the first time felt inclined to believe the Syndicate's promotional literature about the quality of the atmosphere at Heliopolis.

Salah was waiting for him with outstretched hand, some chairs in the shade and a flask of rather good coffee.

'Yes, I've got to see him,' he said. 'They're always breaking out. I know that this time there was an excuse—the wind blew down part of the fencing—but really, we can't go on like this. Suppose a stray one frightened the horses? During a race? I mean, the racing is about to start, and there'll be a lot of money riding on the horses, and you just can't have the whole thing being interrupted by ostriches! We'd become a laughing stock!'

'Does it happen that often?'

'Oh yes. There was one the other day—you saw it, I believe. Malik tried to shoot it. It would have been a good thing if he had. But he had bad luck, I understand. No, they're breaking out all the time. There was another one two or three days before, caused a lot of damage.'

'Well, I suppose it's all part of the mamur's job. At Heliopolis, at any rate.'

Salah laughed.

'Heliopolis is a bit different from the usual district. I quite like it, though. The Syndicate's good to work with. They get on and do things, and that's what this country needs.'

He looked sideways at Owen.

'I'm quite a Nationalist, you know. Not a Party member, of course. I wouldn't go as far as that. That was what you wanted to talk to me about, wasn't it?'

Owen nodded.

'The Syndicate said that it had evidence that some of the workforce were professional agitators. I just wondered how reliable that evidence was.'

'Pretty reliable. It asked me to do a bit of digging, in my spare time. That was before I took up the post here. I checked on the backgrounds of some of the men they mentioned.'

'The man I am interested in is named Wahid. He works in the track-laying gang.'

'I know the man. Yes, he was one of them. I can tell you quite a lot about him. He was one of those who failed the secondary certificate so he couldn't go on to one of the higher colleges. I think he always felt bitter about that, I think that may explain—Anyway, he'd failed and that was that. He had to go into an office as a junior effendi. He went into Public Works.'

'Not Railways?'

'No, no. This was some time ago, five or six years ago. And he went in as an effendi, not as a labourer. He stayed there for about three years and became increasingly dissatisfied. He wasn't getting anywhere, or, at least, not as far as he thought he ought to be getting and he put it down to bias. Anyway, one day, after an argument, he walked out. There's a gap in the record after this. He appears to have done a number of odd jobs, some of them possibly in the docks, for the next time we heard of him, which is when he applied for a job with the electric railway, he produced a reference from a warehouse at Bulak.'

Salah looked at Owen.

'The reference was false. When I checked at the warehouse they'd never heard of him.'

'The company didn't check at the time?'

'They didn't bother. He seemed the sort of man they wanted—experience of hard labour, shifting sacks of grain, that sort of thing.'

'Why did you check the references?'

Salah stared at him.

'Why did I check the references?'

'Him particularly.'

'He was one of several. The company asked me—'

'They picked him out? Why was that, I wonder?'

'Because he was difficult, I suppose.'

'I can understand that. But that doesn't necessarily make him a Nationalist. I'm still looking for evidence of a Nationalist connection.'

'There's plenty of that. He's been seen at Nationalist meetings.'

'So have half the workforce, I imagine.'

'Playing an active part.'

'Doing what?'

'Distributing leaflets.'

'That's more like it. But it hardly makes him a professional agitator.'

'Have you heard him talking to his gang? He's always stirring up trouble!'

'I've no doubt about that. But *professional?* Paid?'

'There's no direct evidence. But—'

Owen was silent. He thought it very likely that Wahid was a Nationalist. He was pretty sure, from what the men had said, that he tried to raise them to action in pursuit of their grievances. But that didn't make him a planted agitator.

'I'd need more evidence of a direct Party connection,' he said, 'before I could be sure that the Nationalists were behind this.'

'There *is* evidence,' Salah insisted.

'Can you produce it?'

'You will have it,' promised Salah.

⁂

Sand had drifted against the fences of the pens, in several places bending them over. Men were working on them to repair them. The ostriches were huddled on the far side of the pens.

The old Arab, Zaghlul, whom Owen had seen on the day of the ostrich hunt, was overseeing the work.

'Yes,' he said impatiently, 'the fences were damaged. What do you expect? Think the sand's going to miss me out?'

'The fences need to be kept in good order,' said Salah sternly. 'Things are not like they used to be!'

'What do you think I'm doing to the fences? And I know things are not the way they used to be; they're a great deal worse!'

'We can't have these birds getting out.'

'Do you think I want them to get out? Each one costs me a packet, I can tell you. That's money walking away, that is. And if they don't get away altogether, some fool tries to shoot them!'

'You go easy on the "fools". We're talking Pashas here!'

'What do I care about Pashas? Or the Khedive either. Put a bullet in my birds and I'll put a bullet in them!'

'These birds of yours are nothing but a nuisance. They frighten the horses. Do you know what a racehorse costs?'

'I know what an ostrich costs. And the birds were here before the racehorses.'

'Yes, well, you keep them on this side of the railway line! Otherwise there'll be trouble.'

'There's been no trouble up till now. It's building this new city that's causing the trouble. City!' said the old man contemptuously. 'What do they want to build a city for out in the desert? The desert's the desert. Keep it like that!'

'Things don't stand still. They're going to build the city and there's nothing you can do about it. You're going to have to live with it. And that means seeing that your birds don't get out.'

'They'd be all right if they were left alone.'

'If they stay in the pens they will be left alone.'

'No, no, it's in the air. They can smell it. It frightens them. That's what makes them panic.'

'What's in the air?'

'People. Houses. That new railway line. The old one's all right. They've got used to that. But now they're building a new one. What do they want another one for? They're building them all over the place. How many more are there going to be?'

'There aren't going to be any more. Just this one. And they're having it because it'll go straight to Heliopolis. It won't come near your pens.'

'There's something wrong with it, isn't there?'

'What do you mean, something wrong with it?'

'It's electric, isn't it?'

'Well?'

'There you are, then. It'll be getting out and affecting my birds.'

'Nonsense!'

'Well, I can tell you, if it starts affecting my birds, I'll be over there with my gun! I'll soon put a stop to it!'

'It won't affect your birds at all.'

'It had better not. And you'd do better to be worrying about all that stuff getting out than about my birds getting out. I'll look after my birds. And I'll look after that new electric railway, too, if you don't watch out!'

Since he was out at Matariya, Owen thought he might as well go over to the village. With any luck he would meet Mahmoud and find out if he had made any further progress.

The village was only a mile from the ostrich farm but by the time he reached it, even in what he had thought the fresher atmosphere of out of town, the sweat was running down his face and his shirt was sticking to his back. When he got to the village he went to the well and scooped water over his face and drank a little from the bucket he had pulled up. It tasted of sand.

There were some women at the well, filling their pitchers. They saw the face he had made and one of them said:

'Here, have some of mine. We got it up before the water was disturbed.'

'It was Miriam who disturbed it,' said one of the other women. 'She let the bucket go in too far.'

'I had to, didn't I?' retorted Miriam angrily. 'I was the last one and you'd got the good water out.'

'Ali should have put the cover over the well,' said the first woman accusingly.

An old man sitting in the shade straightened up.

'I did!' he protested. 'It got underneath. It gets every-where.'

'Well, it does that,' the woman conceded.

'It got into my stew,' said another of the women, 'even though I had the lid on.'

Owen accepted the drink gratefully. The women, as was often the case in the villages, were very chatty. None of them wore veils and no one was particularly abashed at speaking to a man, even a white man. It was the men, thought Owen, who insisted on the forms, so jealous of their wives' honour were they.

Or perhaps it wasn't their wives' honour but their own. That, he thought, was certainly so in the case of those brothers they'd locked up.

Actually, he was uneasy about that. He would have to release them soon. He couldn't hold them forever. That was one of the things he wanted to talk to Mahmoud about. He rather hoped that by now Mahmoud was getting somewhere with his investigations. If he was closing in on someone, especially if, as Owen suspected, the person was one of the brothers, it would make it easier to hold them and to prevent the family of the murdered man from taking the law into their own hands.

Mahmoud emerged from one of the pilgrim's houses, saw Owen and came across to greet him. The women, suddenly self-conscious, picked up their pitchers and went off.

Mahmoud sat down on the parapet of the wall and helped himself to some water.

'Getting anywhere?' asked Owen.

'No. I've just about been through all the houses now and no one's seen or heard anything. No one was out on the night Ibrahim was killed, nor knows anyone else who was out. Well, I can believe that. Once it gets dark, everyone in the village stays at home. But these days, when the nights are hot, they sit outside; and don't tell me that no one, no one in the entire village, saw or heard anything!'

'What might they have heard or seen?'

'Someone going out to the Tree. People at the Tree, talking. They *were* talking, we know that from the goatherd.'

'It's some way from the village, though. And it was dark.'

'I need to know who it was that met Ibrahim that night,' said Mahmoud, frustrated.

'Have you gone through the other village yet, Tel-el-Hasan? Someone might have seen people leaving that.'

'The brothers, you mean?'

'Yes.'

'I've got Asif helping me. He's been through the village.'

'Without any luck?'

'The same thing as here. Villagers,' said Mahmoud, 'will tell you nothing. Not if you're from outside.'

He put the bucket back into the recess.

'Actually,' he said, 'I'm increasingly coming to think that the answer doesn't lie here anyway.'

Chapter 7

'Not here?' said Owen, taken aback.

'Oh, here—the village—is something to do with it. It's where it happened. But it's not here that the meaning lies.'

'The meaning?'

'I see a lot of killings,' said Mahmoud. 'This one has a meaning. The body was put on the line to make a point.'

'What kind of point?'

'I don't know. But I'm beginning to wonder whether it might not be more to do with the railway than it is with the village.'

'You're abandoning the idea of it being a revenge killing?'

'Revenge might be part of it.'

'I don't see how revenge could be part of something else. Isn't it complete in itself?'

Mahmoud was silent. Overhead, in the palms, the doves gurgled contentedly.

'As I see it,' he said at last, 'Ibrahim crops up in two contexts. One of them is the village and there are things here that might have led to his death. But I cannot see why they should have led to his body being placed on the line. That part of it must be explained by something else. And it seems to me that we might find the explanation in the other context in which he crops up: the railway.'

'His body was found there, certainly. Does that count as cropping up?'

'He worked there.'

'But that is incidental, surely?'

'Is it? I have asked myself if it might not be—if I could find any connection between Ibrahim's workplace and his death.'

Owen fanned himself. He was used to Mahmoud's deductive approach. The Parquet lawyers had all been trained in the French tradition of law—the Egyptian legal system was based on that of France—and the French influence extended even to habits of thought.

'And what answers did you get?'

He hoped that Mahmoud wasn't going to allow himself to get distracted. He himself was convinced that the answer lay in the village and he wanted to find it pretty quickly before village law took over.

'It was something the railwaymen said yesterday. About Ibrahim. They said there had been some incident or other when Ibrahim had acted as their spokesman.'

'Well?'

'I'd like to find out more about the incident.'

'It sounded as if it was a dispute about work practices.'

'Precisely.'

'I'm afraid I don't see what you're getting at?'

'I was just wondering if the two could be connected.'

'The dispute and—?'

'The fact that Ibrahim played a leading part in the dispute, and his death.'

Owen was shocked.

'You're surely not suggesting—?'

'I'm not suggesting anything. I'm just saying that the time might have come to take a look at the Syndicate's involvement in all this.'

'But it's not involved! It's just that the body was found on the line that it's building!'

'And that the body was that of a man who'd been prominent in a dispute with it.'

'But the dispute was trivial!'

'We don't know that. It might not have seemed trivial to them. Anything that threatened to slow down progress on the line would have struck them as important, I'd have thought.'

'But you're surely not suggesting that they would go to the lengths of—?'

'I don't know what lengths they might go to. That would be one of the things I would want to find out.'

'But what for? What would be the point?'

'As a warning, perhaps?'

'You think the whole thing was meant as a warning?'

'I think the possibility is worth investigating.'

Owen felt quite shocked. How could Mahmoud even entertain the possibility? The Syndicate bore down hard on its workers, perhaps, but to suppose that a respectable international company would go to those lengths was bizarre!

'Companies don't behave like that,' he said.

'Don't they?'

'No. Not even in Egypt.'

It was the wrong thing to say. Mahmoud's face darkened.

'Perhaps they might,' he said, 'in Egypt. Where they thought it didn't matter.'

Owen backtracked swiftly. Talking to Mahmoud was sometimes like walking through a minefield.

'OK, OK,' he said. 'I'm sorry. I didn't mean it like that. What I meant was that I don't believe a respectable company would do a thing like that anywhere.'

Mahmoud bowed his head in acknowledgement of the apology; stiffly, however.

'Respectable companies don't always behave respectably when they go to other countries,' he said. 'Especially if they're poorer countries.'

Owen felt a tide of exasperation welling up.

'What you're suggesting is quite ridiculous,' he said coldly.

'You may think so.'

'You think so only because it is a foreign company.'

'What are you saying? What are you saying?' cried Mahmoud furiously.

'That you're letting your Nationalist prejudices run away with you!' said Owen, equally angry.

⁕

It had all boiled up, as so often in Egypt, out of nothing. One moment you had been talking reasonably; the next, there had been an explosion.

All right, this time it was he himself who had sparked it off. But really! How could Mahmoud think a thing like that? How could someone as intelligent, as reasonable as Mahmoud even consider such a possibility? Owen had no great affection for the Syndicate. He thought it was hard and grasping. He thought it very likely that it would if not bend the law, at least push up as hard against it as it could.

But that was not quite the same thing as breaking the law. And it was not the same thing as killing a man, or having him killed, just because he had crossed them.

Or as a warning. Warning? Who to? To the labour force to work harder? Ridiculous! How could Mahmoud even suppose such a thing! It was quite unlike him. He was normally the most reasonable of men: a little prickly on occasion, emotional, perhaps, like most Arabs. But this was plain crazy! Companies were not like that. Not even—*pace*, Mahmoud—in Egypt. Not even—despite the fulminations of the most lunatic Nationalists—foreign companies in Egypt. How could Mahmoud even entertain the idea?

The telephone rang. It was Mr Rabbiki, the veteran politician.

'Ah, Captain Owen! So glad you are there. I wanted to let you know before actually putting down the question.'

'Question?'

'Yes. In the Assembly. It's on the agenda for Tuesday. I wanted to give you prior warning. After all, we're old friends, aren't we? And I understand the difficult position you're in. But really, we can't allow this to go on. The poor fellow's family—'

'Poor fellow?'

'The one who was killed. I understand you are not going to press charges?'

'It's not my job to press charges. That's up to the Parquet.'

'Ah, yes, but sometimes they need help.'

'I give them all the help I can.'

'We-ell…it's not always possible, is it?'

'Why not?'

'Political considerations? Do not sometimes political considerations intervene?'

'They haven't intervened in this case.'

'No? That's not the impression I have gained.'

'I don't follow you, Mr Rabbiki.'

'The Syndicate, Captain Owen…is it not obstructing inquiries?'

'Not as far as I'm aware.'

'I understand Mr El Zaki wishes to put some questions?'

'He wanted to talk to the workforce. He asked me to approach the Syndicate on his behalf, which I was glad to do. Permission was given, and he spoke to the men. I was there.'

'Yes, but since then…'

'I don't think the issue has arisen since then.'

There was a little silence.

'Then I am under a false impression, Captain Owen. I had gathered he wished to put some questions about an incident that had happened on the railway some weeks ago.'

'I know the incident to which you refer. I wasn't aware that he wanted to approach the Syndicate over the matter.'

'You weren't? Well, perhaps there are problems of communication on your side. Or perhaps he didn't feel it necessary for an officer of the Ministry of Justice to have to direct his inquiries through an intermediary. Be that as it may, his request was refused.'

'I didn't know that.'

'It is unacceptable, Captain Owen. It raises important questions of principle.'

'It is regrettable, certainly. And the issue might not have arisen had the request been directed through me.'

'But that, too, raises questions of principle, Captain Owen. So you will quite see why we are putting down a question.'

⚜

Owen could quite see why the Nationalist Party was putting down a question. It wished to embarrass the Administration and a foreign company was a good stick to beat the government with.

He was a little disappointed, though, by Mahmoud. After that last exchange at the well, Mahmoud had stalked off in high dudgeon. This was not uncommon with Mahmoud, and usually after a decent interval had elapsed he stalked back again. This time, however, he had made no effort to contact Owen. Instead, he had approached the Syndicate head-on and received the rebuff he must have expected.

Why had he done that? Owen could see why this time he had not wished to enlist his own aid. Apart from understandable pique, he, too, had principles. But why had he gone at it like that? He was no fool, he was wise in the games that Cairo played, he must have known he would get nowhere.

Unless, of course, that was where he had wanted to get. Unless that had been his deliberate intention. Unless he had been party to the Nationalists' decision to exploit the issue for political ends and had seen this, with them, as a heaven-sent opportunity to set the Syndicate up.

Mahmoud was, like all the other Parquet lawyers, himself a Nationalist. Unlike most of them, however, he was also his own man. He made it a matter of principle not to get into politicians' pockets. The law for him was clean and pure and should be above politics. Those who professed it should serve it with independence and austerity. Friends said of him—increasingly—that he was a born judge but too honest to be an advocate. Especially in Cairo.

Owen was surprised, then, to find that in this instance he seemed to have shifted; surprised, and disappointed. He and

Mahmoud had always seen eye to eye, in so far as it was possible for a foreigner to see eye to eye with an Egyptian. But it was precisely that which was raising the difficulty in the present case. For it was surely only the fact that it was foreign that had led Mahmoud to make his extraordinary accusations against the Syndicate.

It was most unlike him. Certainly, like most Nationalists and, indeed, most Egyptians, he chafed at his country's subservience to foreign interests and objected, in particular, to British rule; but up till now he had always been temperate and pragmatic about this, believing that Reason—Mahmoud was a great man for Reason—and the ordinary political processes would in the end deliver Egypt from its foreign yoke. The sanguinary rhetoric of the extremists was not for him.

And yet here he was supposing things about the Belgians which would not have been out of place sixty years before at the court of Muhammed Ali! Muhammed's daughter, taking after her father, had been in the habit of having slave girls who had fallen asleep on duty disembowelled in her bedroom.

It was most unlike him. So unlike him that Owen began to wonder.

⁂

Salah-el-Din took Owen to a little square not far from the Pont de Limoun. There was a fountain in the square and a small crowd had gathered in front of it. Among them, Owen could see the railway workers. They stood in a group, huddled together sheepishly, occasionally casting a longing look over their shoulders at a small café on the other side of the square, as if they would rather have been there than here and as if they might have been tempted to make a bolt for it had they not been hemmed in.

It was a hot evening and most of the little houses in the square had their front doors open. From the yards at the back came drifting the smell of charcoal and burning cooking fat, and then a very pungent smell of fried onions.

One or two of the households had already finished their evening meal and had come out to sit on their doorsteps, trying to catch a breath of cooler air. They called across to the men sitting on the big stone bench, the *mastaba*, that ran along the front of the café. Other men were sitting on the ground in front of them. Mixed with the smell of charcoal and fat came now a strong smell of coffee.

Darkness fell quickly at this time of year. Already people in the crowd were lighting torches. On the side of the square opposite the café the dome of a mosque was beginning to show against the sky.

There was the sound of singing in one of the side streets and then a small procession came into the square carrying cresset torches, long staves with bits of burning wood attached to them, and chanting slogans.

They marched up to the fountain and pushed through the crowd. The men with torches gathered around the base of the fountain. Owen could see now that the water had been turned off. A man began to climb up on to the base.

It was dark now in the square. Only the café was lit up. The dome of the mosque was very clear against a deep-blue velvety sky. There was a little group of men standing in front of its doors, the local imam, probably, with some of his helpers.

The men at the fountain held their cressets up to illuminate the speaker on the plinth. He wore a dark suit and a tarboosh. Apart from one or two of the men who had come with him, no one else in the crowd wore a tarboosh. They were all in galabe-ahs, the long, dress-like costume of the ordinary Cairo working man, and skull caps.

That was how it was, thought Owen. The Nationalist Party drew almost all its strength from office workers and from the professional classes. They hardly touched ordinary working people. There was as big a gulf between them and the ordinary people of Egypt as there was between the ruling Pashas and most educated Egyptians. Egypt was a country divided among itself.

The man on the plinth began to speak. It was the usual Nationalist line. The rich were assailed, foreigners were attacked. But it was a man in a suit who was speaking and the crowd listened for the most part in silence.

Here, though, suddenly, was something different. The speaker began to talk about the railway. Railways were good, he said. It was through railways that a modern Egypt would be built. But why did they have to be built by foreigners? Were there no Egyptians who could build them?

But, pardon him, he had made a mistake. They *were* built by Egyptians, by people like those he could see before him in the crowd below. It was Egyptian hands that laid the tracks. But was it Egyptian people who got the money? Was it Egyptian mouths that got the bread? No, it was foreign mouths that got the bread. Only it wasn't bread they wanted, it was cake! With icing on it! The Egyptians did the work but it was the foreigners who benefited.

And it was hard work! His friends down below him could testify to that. It was hard work, back-breaking work. And now they were about to heap more on weary shoulders! Had they not heard about the straw that broke the camel's back? And this was no straw that they were piling on. No, indeed.

Their hearts went out to their weary brothers. They would not struggle alone. The country was with them. There was action they could take and if they took it, they would find they were not without friends. No, indeed.

But this time the foreigners had overreached themselves. Not content with oppressing their workers, they seemed determined now to offend everyone else. An insult to religion was an insult to all Egyptians. God's Day was holy; and Egyptians, he said, raising his voice for the benefit of those gathered on the steps in front of the mosque, were determined to keep it holy!

He waited for the cheers, and indeed they came, but not exactly enthusiastically. The little group before the mosque did not join in. If there was a gap between the Nationalists and the ordinary Cairene, there was an even wider gap between the Nationalists and the Church. The Nationalist Party was predominantly secular. They were a modernizing party and modernizing, for many of them, meant sweeping away much of the influence of the Church.

Which the Church knew very well. The imam would have spotted this tactic a mile off. Even so, thought Owen, it might be worth keeping an eye on how successful the tactic was. Ordinary people might be less discriminating than the imam and if the Nationalists could add religious fervour to popular hostility then they could make a lot of trouble.

The orator, as was the way with Arab orators, continued for another hour or two before bringing his final peroration to a close. His friends helped him to climb down. In the light of the cresset torches Owen could see them clearly. As the party prepared to move off, one of the men talking to the speaker turned and Owen saw his face. It was Wahid. Not the Wahid of the railway line, in skull cap and galabeah, and begrimed with sweat, but a Wahid in the sharp, cheap suit and tasselled tarboosh of the smart, young, Nationalist effendi.

'Satisfied?' said Salah-el-Din.

✺

Unexpectedly, Owen received a request from Mahmoud to hold the three brothers for a few days longer. He was rather relieved. The brothers had been on his conscience. It was all very well holding them in their own best interests—he was fairly convinced that if they were released Ibrahim's family would take a pot-shot at them—but it was hard to justify in terms of law. Something must have turned up for Mahmoud to be making this request.

It meant, too, that Mahmoud must still be working on the village end. Owen had feared, from what Mahmoud had said the last time they had met, that he was about to shift his attention entirely to the Syndicate end—if Syndicate end there was.

Cheered by the thought that things were moving, he rang up Mahmoud to say that of course he would continue to hold the brothers if that was what Mahmoud wanted. Mahmoud, caught off guard by the call, tried to remain distant but found it hard when Owen was being so conciliatory.

'You're getting somewhere, then?'

'Yes.' Mahmoud hesitated. 'I think so. Do you need grounds for holding?'

'I'll take your word for it.'

This, from the point of view of keeping his distance, made matters worse for Mahmoud. What made it even more difficult was that Mahmoud himself had doubts about the strict legality of holding the men further. They were being held under powers special to the Mamur Zapt. Mahmoud, on principle, did not believe the Mamur Zapt should have such powers. They were not assigned him in the Legal Code; and for Mahmoud the Code was Bible—or, possibly, Koran.

However, he was rather glad of the powers on this occasion, for he was not at all sure that holding the brothers could be justified by the normal letter of the law.

'I ought to give you grounds,' he said determinedly.

'Fine!'

Mahmoud hesitated.

'Unfortunately, it is not quite straightforward.'

'Like to talk to me about it?'

'That might be a good idea,' said Mahmoud, relieved. Not all legal considerations, after all, had to be written down.

They met, as usual, on neutral ground, at a café halfway between the Ministry of Justice and Owen's office at the Bab-el-Khalk. It was an Arab café and outside it were several little white asses, waiting for their owners. Inside, water-pipes were bubbling. Neither Owen nor Mahmoud, however, were smoking men, Owen from inclination, Mahmoud out of Muslim conviction. Today he felt slightly relieved at his strictness. Any more relaxing of rules would have made him feel very uneasy.

'Well, what have you found?' said Owen, sipping his coffee.

'I need a little more time,' said Mahmoud, 'but I think I've got it.'

'Got what?'

'The connection. You remember,' he said, 'that I was looking for a connection with the Syndicate. Well, I think I've found it.'

Owen listened with sinking heart. Was Mahmoud still on that tack?

'I had hoped you had found out something more in the village,' he said. 'I mean, if we're going to justify holding them—'

'But that's it,' said Mahmoud, bending forward earnestly, 'that is what I *have* found. A connection between the brothers and the Syndicate. One of the brothers, Ali, his name is, hangs around at the Helwan racetrack a lot. He's in with a gang there.'

'Well, that's interesting. But what has it got to do with—?'

'The Syndicate's building a racetrack out at Heliopolis.'

'Well?'

'Gambling's important to them.'

'I know that. They've applied for a licence to open a saloon at the hotel they're building there.'

'They're opening the racetrack very soon. Even before they've finished building.'

'They need the cash, I think.'

'I think so, too,' said Mahmoud. 'I think they need it badly.'

Owen looked at him.

'You're not suggesting they need it badly enough to kill a man, are you?'

'I'm suggesting that it's pretty important to them to get the railway line to Heliopolis finished as soon as possible.'

Owen could see how from Mahmoud's point of view it all fitted together. All the same…!

'Aren't you jumping the gun a bit? You haven't even succeeded in connecting the brothers with the killing yet.'

'I'm working on that.'

'You need to do that before you start worrying about other connections.'

Mahmoud pursed his lips obstinately.

'I need to work on both. It's not just the killing that has to be explained, but the fact that the body was placed on the line.'

'You're still on that?'

'In my view it is the key.'

'You don't think it could all be explained simply as a revenge killing?'

He couldn't keep the exasperation out of his voice. Mahmoud sensed it and reacted strongly.

'I think it would be very convenient if it were explained as a revenge killing. For some people.'

'Meaning?'

'Such as the Syndicate.'

'For goodness' sake!'

Owen fought to keep his irritation down.

'There are so many gaps! Between the brothers and the killing; between the brothers and the Syndicate. You say he hangs out with a gang; well, between the gang and the Syndicate, too. Gaps, gaps! Everywhere!'

'You see gaps; I see connections. Why was the body placed on the line?'

'How the hell do I know?'

'You're not being very rational.'

'Me? Not being very rational? Well, at least I'm not prejudiced!'

'What is this talk of prejudice?' said Mahmoud furiously.

'The only reason why you're involving the Syndicate at all is because they're foreign!'

'You think it is just that I am a Nationalist, is that it?'

'I think the Nationalist involvement in this needs some explaining.'

'What exactly do you mean by that?'

'Wahid—the railwaymen's leader—is a Nationalist agitator. Why was he put there?'

'"Put there"?'

'He was planted. To make sure that the opportunity was not missed.'

'What "opportunity"?'

'To make things difficult for the government. It's nothing to do with the Syndicate. It's everything to do with the government—and with the Nationalists!'

Mahmoud rose from the table.

'You would think that!' he spat.

Chapter 8

The reception at the Heliopolis Racing Club coincided with the opening of their racing programme, and from the big window Owen could look down on the crowd milling at the starting gate. Milling, certainly, because that was what Cairo crowds always did, move round and round in a mass, getting nowhere. Crowd, more doubtfully, since although there were several score at the finishing post, there were only several dozen at the starting gate and in between there was virtually nobody.

'Promising, though,' said the Belgian beside him. 'As soon as we get the railway line finished they'll come flocking in.'

There was almost more of a crowd upstairs at the reception. The international community had turned out in large numbers. Almost every consulate was represented. The British Consul-General was not there, but Paul, his aide-de-camp and Owen's tennis partner, was standing in for him. Garvin, the Commandant of Police was there, always a man for the races. Princes and Pashas were there in abundance.

Zeinab had also deigned to come. Not because she was in the slightest interested in horses—she knew they pulled her carriage and that was about it—but because she had decided that Owen could not safely be left alone with 'that girl'.

And, indeed, Salah-el-Din's daughter was present, dressed, as always, incongruously to Owen's eye, in a frock which suggested the little girl but somehow revealed a full womanly figure.

'Disgusting!' said Zeinab.

'A bit bizarre!' Owen conceded.

'What do you know about it?' demanded Zeinab.

Owen knew absolutely nothing about women's fashion, which he imagined was what Zeinab was talking about, so decided to keep his mouth shut.

Among the Pashas was Zeinab's father, Nuri, who came up to Owen with a worried look.

'Do you think she'll do it?'

'Do what?'

Nuri jerked his head in the direction of the window where Malik was standing with some of his cronies.

'Kill him, you mean?' Owen considered. 'I wouldn't have thought so,' he said.

Salah-el-Din brought his daughter up to Owen.

'You remember Amina?'

'Charmed!'

'Do you race, Captain Owen?' she asked.

'I ride a bit.'

'Ah! So do I. You must ride out in this direction one morning.'

'I haven't been doing much riding lately,' he said hastily.

'You must take it up again. You used to ride in England?'

'In India.'

'You have been to India? Oh, I would like to go to India. It must be very romantic. You have seen the Taj Mahal, yes?'

'Well, no, actually. I was stationed up in the north.'

'On the Frontier?'

'Yes, as a matter of fact.'

'You were a soldier? You actually fought people?'

'Well—'

'And burned villages? And raped the women?'

'Oh, yes. Every day.'

Amina looked at him wide-eyed.

Across the room Zeinab was talking to Paul. She caught Owen's eye and ostentatiously turned her back.

Malik came up and Amina moved away.

'That's your girlfriend, isn't it?' he said, looking at Zeinab.

'Yes.'

'She looks a bit Arabic to me. Ever tried a Circassian? I could get you one if you'd like an exchange.'

'No, thanks,' said Owen. He made his way over to Paul and Zeinab.

'Who's that strange girl you were talking to?' asked Paul.

'Salah-el-Din's daughter. He's the local mamur.'

'She seems a bit young,' said Paul doubtfully.

Zeinab went off in a fury.

Paul looked down at the scanty crowd below.

'They'll have to do better than this,' he said. 'Of course, it'll be different when they've got the railway finished.'

'I hadn't realized how important it was to them.'

'Oh, it's important, all right.'

'How important?' said Owen.

'Well, it would make a big difference to their cash flow, which, I understand, is a bit sticky—'

'Important enough to kill for?'

Paul stared at him.

'Are you feeling all right? Not been standing out in the sun too long?'

A little later, Owen was talking to one of the undersecretaries when Raoul, the Belgian he had met at Salah-el-Din's, touched him on the arm.

'Still on the bubbly? Care for something harder? Oh, and by the way, el-Sayid Ahmad would like a word with you.'

El-Sayid Ahmad was the Minister for Transport. He stretched out his hand.

'Glad to see you. Impressive, isn't it? A city arising out of nothing. That's the modern Egypt for you!'

He took Owen confidentially aside.

'You know a question has been put down in the Assembly?'

'By Mr Rabbiki, yes.'

'Up to his usual tricks. But you don't have to worry. We'll fob him off.'

'He may be calling for a public inquiry.'

'He won't get one. We have a safe majority. All the same—'

'Yes?'

'He'll get what he wants. Which is public attention.'

'There's not much we can do about that.'

'Isn't there? How near an arrest are you?'

Owen hesitated.

'Faltering?'

'It's in the hands of the Parquet.'

'And they are not pursuing it as zealously as they might? My dear fellow, you don't have to say a word.' He took Owen by the arm, as Arabs always did when they wished to move towards intimacy, and drew him close. '*Entre nous*, the Khedive is most unhappy. Dragging their feet, he said; that's what they're doing! And, of course, that's just what they *are* doing. Nationalists to a man.'

'Minister, you're not suggesting that they could be acting in concert with the Party in the House on this matter?'

'I'm not suggesting anything. But we do have our suspicions. There have been rumours of a big Nationalist move. And it could involve the railway.'

'Why would that make it big?'

'Funds, my boy, it's all to do with funds. Funds from abroad requiring a return on investment, funds for the government—a budget balance, my dear boy, you can't believe how important that is, to some people, anyway. Funds for the Khedive, although naturally that is a minor consideration. All put in jeopardy if the railway is delayed. Big? My dear fellow, I can't say how important it is!'

'Important enough to kill for?'

'You don't need to go that far. Arrest will do. Just something to show that action has been taken.'

'No, no, I wasn't thinking—I meant on the Nationalist side. Important enough for them to kill for?'

'Kill? My dear fellow!'

'I just wondered—'

'Kill! What can you be thinking of! Our colleagues, the Nationalists? My dear fellow! We're not savages, you know. We leave killing to the English.'

El-Sayid Ahmad withdrew his arm and turned away. Raoul appeared with a salver on which were several tumblers of whisky.

'I'll have one of those,' said Garvin, standing nearby. He reached out a hand. 'What was he on about?' he said to Owen.

'The railway; he wants me to hurry it along.'

'Best keep out of it. That's my advice. Have nothing to do with business. Not in Egypt. Or anywhere else, for that matter. Cheers!'

'Cheers! I wish I could. But you can't keep money out of things.'

Garvin peered out of the window.

'Hello!' he said. 'Isn't that some of my old friends?'

He was looking at a group of singularly rough, tough, battered and scarred individuals.

'Where do they come from?' asked Owen.

'Helwan. I've seen them on the racetrack there!'

Garvin had an unrivalled knowledge of all the gangs.

'What are they doing here?'

'I don't know. I'd better find out.'

They were talking to a man in a suit.

'Who's that?'

'One of the stewards, I think,' said Owen.

'Already?' said Garvin. 'I'll have to have a word with the managers.'

'Don't do that,' said Owen. 'Not just yet.'

Garvin moved away to talk to one of the Ministers. Owen decided he had been neglecting Zeinab.

'She's over there,' said Zeinab.

'Who is?'

Away in a corner Salah-el-Din's daughter was surrounded by a ring of Pashas.

'They're even older than you are,' said Zeinab.

Owen at last realized what was bothering her.

'I prefer experience,' he said.

'She's got plenty of that.'

'I doubt it.'

'You're really stupid,' said Zeinab.

Malik went up to join the group.

'He made me an offer to exchange you for a Circassian,' said Owen.

'Did you accept?'

Nuri, who had been one of the ring of Pashas, detached himself and came across to them, puffing with pleasure.

'Charming girl!' he said. 'I like them fresh.'

Zeinab went off in a huff. Nuri looked after her in bewilderment, then, as Owen was about to set out in pursuit, laid a hand on his arm.

'My dear boy,' he said; 'a word with you!'

'Yes?' said Owen, edging after Zeinab.

'Don't do it!'

Owen stopped, surprised.

'Not even for her! Believe me, I know what I'm talking about. There was a time—I cared just as passionately as you. And there was this other man. Well, I said to her—it was Zeinab's mother, you know—you can have him. If you like cold meat! I meant it, too, you know. I would have killed him. Or perhaps I did kill him? I can't remember now, it was so long ago. Anyway, it brought us back together again. Passionate women like passion. You English are too—wait a minute, where was I? No, no, I meant it the other way round! My boy,' said Nuri impressively, 'you must not kill him!'

'Kill who?' asked Owen, totally confused.

'Malik.'

'Why not?' demanded Zeinab, drawn back.

'Because he's betrothed, or nearly betrothed, to that charming girl. Abu Hanafi was telling me. His father objects, of course, but—'

'Is that why you wanted to kill him?' said Zeinab dangerously.

'I don't want to kill anyone!' protested Owen.

'He let it slip,' said Nuri, 'when he was talking to el-Sayid Ahmad. El-Sayid Ahmad was shocked. "These English!" he said. "They will fall upon you like beasts!" "It's only instinct," I said. "He's young and passionate. I was just the same. He's not going to let another man step in, is he?" "Yes, but to go so far as to kill him!" said el-Sayid Ahmad. "It is a bit far," I conceded. So I said I would have a word with you.'

'Was it when he offered to exchange me for a Circassian?' said Zeinab fondly.

'Whisky, sir?' said the waiter, going past.

'A double, please,' said Owen.

❧

'There is a problem about the Tree,' said McPhee worriedly.

'Tree?'

'The Tree of the Virgin. The French want to take possession of it.'

'Just a minute,' said Owen; 'the French? What the hell's it got to do with them?'

'It was given to the Empress Eugenie by the Khedive when she came for the opening of the Suez Canal.'

'Yes, I know, but—'

'Along with the Gezira Palace Hotel.'

'They don't want the hotel as well, do they?'

'They haven't said so. It seems it's just the Tree they want. Because of the Roman Catholic connections.'

'*Roman Catholic?*'

'It's the balsam, you see.'

'I thought you told me it was a sycamore? Or a fig?'

'No, no, it's the shrubs nearby. They're balsam—'

'Where that old goatherd was?'

'Yes. They used to provide the balsam for nearly all the baptismal services in Egypt. Every Catholic child!'

'Let's get this straight,' said Owen, who was feeling fragile this morning anyway and was still trying to digest everything that had happened to him at the reception. 'They want the Tree because of the balsam shrubs nearby?'

'They'd like the shrubs, of course. But, strictly speaking, it was only the Tree of the Virgin that was given them. I think you could make a stand on that.'

'I'm not making a stand on anything. Certainly not on a bloody tree!'

'I do think you ought to consult Diplomatic, Owen. The request comes from the Quai d'Orsay.'

'In Paris? How the hell did they get to know about it?'

'I think'—McPhee lowered his voice, not wishing to speak ill, or, at least, ill loudly of anybody—'I think it may have got to them through the Syndicate. The Belgians—or, at least, some of them—are RCs, too, you know.'

'But why—?'

'Well, if the Tree was gone, you know, it would be, well, gone. Out of the way. Didn't you tell me it was in the way of the new railway?'

'Yes, but—you don't mean they'd take it away to France?'

'Well, why not? After all, we've taken Cleopatra's Needle to London.'

'Yes, but that's a—I mean, this is a tree! It's even dead. Do they know it's dead? It's fallen down.'

'That makes it easier to take it away. All they have to do is lift it on to a lorry. In any case, Owen, I don't think you should assume too readily that it's dead. I'm sure I saw green shoots. And, even if it were dead, Owen, that's not the important thing.'

'No?'

'No. The thing is, it has symbolic life. It's very important to RCs, Owen. The Young Mother is said to have rested in its shade. Then she took the Child, hot and weary from the journey, down to the well and bathed it; and instantly the water became fresh and clean. I must say, I do think that is a point we have to consider. I mean, the water *is* strikingly fresh and clean and all the other wells round there are rather salty. How is that to be explained?'

'Well—'

'And then, while the Child was capering about, or perhaps just lying there, she washed its clothes. I mean, that's what they often do, you see them doing that today, then the child can put them on again. But then, do you know, when she wrung the clothes out, wherever the drops of water fell, balsam trees sprang out of the earth! So you see, in fact there *is* a connection between the Virgin Tree and the balsam—'

'I think that point may be disputed.'

'The lawyers may well make a meal of it, I know, but symbolically—'

'Yes. Well. I'm sure. And you say'—grasping at straws—'that this has come formally from the French Consulate?'

'Direct from the Ministry in Paris, they said.'

'Ah, well, then,' said Owen. 'I'm afraid I shall have to refer this to our own Consulate.'

⁕

Back came the answer, sooner than he had wished.

'We've referred it to our lawyers,' said Paul.

'Great!'

'They've warned us that it could take some time.'

'Marvellous!'

'However, they have suggested that you put a guard on the Tree.'

'How long for?'

'Until the issue is resolved.'

'How long could that be?'

'Ten years.'

⁕

'No, the British are not seizing your property. The guard is there merely to protect it.'

'It's been all right for two thousand years,' said the Copt. 'Why does it suddenly need protection?'

Owen pointed to the names carved on the bark.

'It's being defaced.'

'That's how I make my money,' protested Daniel indignantly.

'Ah, yes. But you shouldn't. Not while ownership of the property is being disputed.'

'It's not being disputed. It's mine.'

'Apparently it was given to the Empress Eugenie in 1869.'

'This is a Muslim plot!' cried Daniel, reeling back.

'The Muslims are nothing to do with it,' said Owen sternly. He wasn't going to have this adding fuel to the fire.

ഗ‌‌‌ཙ‌

Or so he thought.

'A deputation to see you,' announced Nikos, his Official Clerk.

'Deputation?'

'From the Patriarch.'

The outer office was full of Copts.

'This is outrageous!' said their leader, one of three bishops.

'What exactly—?'

'The seizing of Coptic property.'

'Ah, the Tree? I have explained that the guard is there merely to protect it.'

'It certainly needs protection; but who from?'

'Well—'

'First you let the Muslims defile it. Then you let the Catholics take it away!'

'We're really not at that stage yet.'

'Ah! Then it is true? The Catholics are going to take it at some time?'

'The Tree, apparently, was a gift to the Empress Eugenie—'

'Yes, but who gave it?'

'The Khedive Ismail—'

'But did it belong to him?' Seeing his advantage, the bishop pressed home. 'Was it his to give?'

'Well, I—'

'It has belonged to Copts for over a thousand years.'

'Look, this is a matter for lawyers—'

'One would think so. But the judgement has, apparently, already been made.'

'Not at all.'

'Why, then, has a guard been placed at the Tree?'

'To protect it pending a resolution of the issue. Until then the assumption is that ownership remains as it is at present.'

'We demand that the rights of Coptic citizens be protected!'

'I give you that assurance.'

'What is it worth, though?' asked one of the other bishops. 'Will Britain stand up for Copts the way France does for Roman Catholics?'

'The policy of His Majesty's government is not to interfere in religious matters. In the case of Egypt, it has consistently urged the Khedive not to discriminate against particular groups of his subjects—'

'He has given away our Tree!'

<hr />

When Owen next visited the Tree he found not just the guard he had posted but also six other men.

'Who are they?'

'Friends,' said Daniel, grinning.

They were all Copts. Copts tended to be small. These weren't.

'What are they doing here?'

'Helping to protect the Tree. You said it needed protection.'

Owen had managed to arrive just before Sheikh Isa. The sheikh descended from his donkey and looked at the men.

'Who are these men?' he said.

'My assistants,' said Daniel.

'What do you need assistants for?'

'To hold the knives. See?'

The men produced daggers from their clothes and brandished them ostentatiously.

'We'll have no trouble!' Owen warned.

'Trouble? This is just in case anyone wants to carve their name. A knife is available at a fee. And without one, if that's absolutely necessary.'

'This is a Muslim tree,' said Sheikh Isa.

'You reckon?' said one of the Copts.

'The ownership is under dispute,' said Owen, 'and will be settled in the courts.'

'So you don't own it then?' cried Sheikh Isa.

'I certainly do,' retorted Daniel. 'And no Frenchman is going to take it away from me.'

'Frenchman?' said Sheikh Isa, bewildered.

'The Tree was given to the Empress Eugenie,' Owen explained. 'Or so the French say.'

'Frenchmen? Foreigners?' said Sheikh Isa incredulously.

'Catholics!' spat Daniel. 'They're all Catholics!'

'Christians? Not more Christians!' cried Sheikh Isa.

'They're not taking my Tree away!' said Daniel.

'Take it away?'

'No one's taking it away,' said Owen, intervening swiftly. 'The French have just made a claim for it, that's all. It will be settled in the courts.'

'It will be settled on the battlefield!' shouted Sheikh Isa. 'Take it away? The desert will run with blood first!'

⊙〜〜⊙

The next day, in addition to the guard and the six Copts, there were another six men.

'Who are you?' said Owen.

'We are Sheikh Isa's men. The Sons of Islam.'

'What are you doing here?'

'Looking after the Tree. The Catholics are coming to take it away. These Copt bastards are going to give it to them.'

'I'm going to give it to you!' said Daniel, getting to his feet.

'Cut it out!' snapped Owen. 'Any nonsense from any of you and you'll all be in the *caracol!* You!' he said to the guard. 'See there's no trouble!'

'What, me?' said the guard. 'On my own?'

The next day, in addition to the guard, the six Copts and the six Sons of Islam, there were three other guards.

'Four men?' said Garvin, the Commandant of Police, whose men they were. 'For how long? How long did you say it was going to be before the case was decided?'

⊙〰〰〰⊙

The village was got up as if for a festival. Banners were hung across the street, bunting festooned all the houses. Holy texts dangled from the windows.

'What's all this?' said Owen to his friend the barber.

'It's the pilgrims,' said the barber. 'Any day now they'll start arriving.'

'On their way to Birket-el-Hadj?'

'That's right. It's where they all gather.'

Owen frowned. He had forgotten about the Mecca caravan.

'They pass through here?'

'And through the other villages. They come from all sides.'

Owen's frown deepened. The last thing he could do with just at the moment was hordes of the devout converging on the neighbourhood.

'When does the caravan leave?'

'Oh, not for several weeks yet. It takes time for them all to assemble.'

Sheikh Isa stood at the door of his house.

'Is there not joy in your heart, Englishman?' he demanded, gesturing at all the decorations.

Not a lot, thought Owen. Out loud he said:

'It is always a pleasure to see the signs of joy.'

'There is joy in our hearts. For this is the time when the faithful gather to make the Great Journey.'

'Happiness, indeed,' said Owen, bowing his head politely. 'We rejoice with them.'

'Quite so!'

'But mutedly.'

'Mutedly?' said Owen.

'For three reasons.'

Owen tried to edge past.

'First,' said the sheikh determinedly, 'because they are only on their outward way. Their hearts have not yet felt the holy touch. It is only on the return journey that their joy, and ours, knows no end.'

'Joy, indeed!'

'Second, however,' said Sheikh Isa, 'our joy is limited because we think of those who do not travel with them.'

'Ah, the sadness!' murmured Owen sympathetically.

'Backsliders!' shouted Sheikh Isa. 'Backsliders, all of them! The faint of heart in the villages! The godless in the infidel towns! Snakes, vermin, worse than vermin; Christians! Worse than Christians; Copts!'

'Yes, well—'

'The third reason,' said Sheikh Isa inexorably, 'why our joy is muted is this: the caravan is no longer what it was. Each year the numbers are fewer.'

He looked accusingly at Owen.

'They are going by train, perhaps,' suggested Owen helpfully.

This was a mistake. Sheikh Isa glared at him.

'That,' he said harshly, 'is where the error begins.'

Owen continued to edge away.

'The world changes,' he said, 'and we must change with it.'

'Not so!' bellowed Sheikh Isa. 'If we are tempted, do we have to fall? The railway is put there to tempt us; do we have to yield? The devil builds a city; do we have to go to it?'

'I wouldn't if I were you,' said Owen.

Sheikh Isa stared into the distance.

'But what,' he almost whispered, 'if it comes to me? What if the railway creeps across the desert towards me? What if it enters the village and lures the hearts of the foolish people with gold? What if the devil's houses reach out to touch my own? What do I do then?'

Chapter 9

Owen's offering to pay for Ja'affar's treatment had made him a friend if not of the whole village, then very definitely of the barber and, as he went past, the barber hailed him and invited him to take tea. The chair was empty for the moment, no chins requiring shaving, no injuries, treatment and no penises, circumcision, and the barber was free to bustle about preparing tea for his cronies.

Owen joined the ring squatting on the ground. One of the ring was Ja'affar.

'How's it going, Ja'affar?'

'Terribly. I'll soon have to go back to work.'

'Old man Zaghlul was round after him this morning,' volunteered one of the others.

'The old bastard! He's worse than the Belgians!' said Ja'affar indignantly.

'He'll be in the village every day now for a bit. He'll be keeping his eye on you!'

Owen settled back and let the tide of conversation flow over him.

'I saw Zaghlul just now,' said someone.

'Yes, he's talking to Sheikh Isa.'

'What's he talking about?'

'It'll be to do with the pilgrims.'

'Don't tell me he's trying to sell them ostriches!'

'No, no. Camels. Some of them will need new camels for the journey. He can get them from his friends in the desert.'

'Those thieving Bedouin! I bet he makes a piastre or two!'

'You know what? I've heard they sell them to the pilgrims here and then steal them back later.'

'And I wouldn't be surprised if that old man Zaghlul had a hand in both, the murderous old skinflint!'

'What happens?' asked Owen. 'Does Sheikh Isa go over to the Birket-el-Hadj and take orders?'

'More or less. He's over there most days at this time of year and no doubt he keeps his ears open. If he gets to hear of someone wanting camels he lets Zaghlul know about it.'

'Old Zaghlul's in the mosque most mornings now. It's amazing how devout he gets when the pilgrims are around!'

'Well, that was how he made his fortune wasn't it? Supplying the pilgrims.'

'That was in the old days. These days he's into ostriches. Got out at the right time, too, I'd say. Once that new town gets built, the storekeepers there will have their eyes on the Birket-el-Hadj.'

'They'll have their eyes on richer people than pilgrims, if what I hear is true.'

'What do you hear?' asked Owen.

'That Heliopolis is going to be for the rich.'

'The poor will get shouldered out,' said the barber. 'That's always the way of it.'

'Old man Zaghlul will get shouldered out, from what I hear. Ostriches and horses don't mix.'

'He won't like that,' said Ja'affar.

'It'll be for the second time, too. He won't take that lying down.'

'He's in the wrong place, that's the trouble. The rich have got their eye on it and the rich always get what they want.'

'We're in the wrong place, too. And do you know why? Because they're not building out on our side. If they were, we could be doing very well for ourselves. They'd be offering us money for our land like they're doing in Tel-el-Hasan.'

'Tel-el-Hasan? That's where that Copt comes from. I'll bet *he's* doing all right!'

'He's doing all right anyway. What with that Tree!'

'Ah, but he won't have the Tree much longer. They're going to take it away.'

'Take it away? They must be crazy!'

'Well, they *are* crazy. They're foreigners. That's right, isn't it?' he appealed to Owen.

'Some foreigners do want to take it away. But it won't happen.'

'Take the Tree away! Whatever next!'

'It won't happen,' said Owen, 'at least, not for years.'

'One day, though, it will,' said the barber. 'That's it, you see. Everything's changing. You think things are going to go on forever as they are and then one day they start building a town and the next thing you know there's a massive town on your doorstep, and it spreads and spreads—one day, you mark my words, there'll be houses from here to Cairo!'

'Oh, come on!'

'Ridiculous!'

'You're letting yourself be carried away, Suleiman!'

'Houses all the way from here to Cairo,' repeated the barber, highly satisfied at the effect of this conjuring up of the Apocalypse.

'You don't think so, do you?' they appealed to Owen.

'Houses all the way to Cairo? No!'

'I don't think so either,' said one of the men. 'And do you know why? Because before the houses get to Cairo, they'll get to Birket-el-Hadj. And there they'll stop.'

'Why?' asked the barber.

'Don't be daft, Suleiman. Because that's where the pilgrims are. That's where the caravan starts.'

'So?'

'They're not going to change that, are they?'

'Well—' began the barber.

But his words were lost in the chorus of disbelief and disapproval.

For Owen, squatting on the sand, drinking the bitter, black, but oddly refreshing tea of the fellahin, listening to the creak of the sagiya from the well and the gurgles of the doves in the palms, the sounds and tastes and sensations of Egypt immemorial, it seemed inconceivable too.

Yet the railway was stretching over the desert and the houses were being built. The world was changing, as he had so glibly said to Sheikh Isa. For perhaps the first time he realized fully how it must appear to the villagers, how it must appear to Isa, and felt a twinge of sympathy.

'Sheikh Isa does not like it,' he said.

'He does not.'

'He hasn't liked it from the first,' said someone, 'not from the day Ibrahim said he was going to work for them. He had us all in and said it was the devil's work we'd be doing. But Ibrahim said it was just like any other work and that he needed the money. Several others thought that, too. Sheikh Isa was very angry and said that it would be on our own heads.'

'So you didn't go, Mohammed?'

'They wouldn't have me. I'm glad now. He was right, wasn't he? Look what happened to Ibrahim.'

'That's nothing to do with it!' said the barber. 'What happened to Ibrahim happened because he was fooling around with other women and got across those mad brothers of his wife. I always said he shouldn't have married out of the village!'

'Not to someone from Tel-el-Hasan, anyway,' said Ja'affar. 'There's always trouble when you mix with that lot.'

'Yes, but it wouldn't have happened if God hadn't willed it,' said Mohammed, unwilling to relinquish his position.

The free-thinking barber, however, would have none of it.

'God's got better things to do than breaking Ibrahim's neck,' he said firmly.

Owen, listening soporifically in the sun, and slipping ever deeper into the villagers' world, was becoming more and more convinced that the answer to the riddle of Ibrahim's death lay here in the village and not in the city. Mahmoud could look there if he wished.

⌒⇜⌒

A violent tooting disturbed the slumbers of the houses.

'What's that?' said Owen, startled.

'It'll be the Pasha's son,' said someone.

'Come to see Jalila,' said the barber.

A motor car—*the* motor car—nosed its way into the street with a horde of urchins running alongside. It came to a stop beside the barber's.

'Hello, Owen!' called Malik.

Owen got to his feet.

'Thirsty? I wouldn't drink that stuff. It's the water, you know. Best avoided. I've got something better here. Fancy a drop?'

'No, thanks. Not while I'm working.'

'Working? Here? What on?'

'It's the case of that chap who was found on the line.'

'The villager? But my dear fellow, you don't bother about villagers! They're always killing each other. Leave them to it, is my motto.'

'Ah, yes, but, you see, it was interfering with work on the line.'

'Oh, *that* fellow! Damned nuisance. Why they didn't just push him off and get on with it I can't understand. But, my dear chap, you shouldn't be concerning yourself with this sort of thing! Leave that to the Parquet. What you ought to be doing is seeing that the Nationalists don't exploit it.'

'Well, thanks.'

'They're only too ready, you know.'

'Yes, I'm sure.'

'Stick to essentials, that's my advice.'

'Thank you. And you: sticking to essentials, too?'

Malik laughed.

'I'm over here to see a woman, if that's what you mean. But I wouldn't call her essential. Not in particular, that is. Just women in general.'

'And none nearer at hand? But, Malik, how sad!'

'There are plenty nearer at hand,' said Malik, offended. 'I just happened to be passing, that's all.'

'All the same, I'm surprised you think her worth your attention.'

'A mere village woman, you mean? Well, you know, she has her points.'

'I must confess, though, Malik, I *am* a little surprised. Someone like you! Sharing her with the villagers!'

Malik looked at him.

'You know about that?' he said, slightly disconcerted. 'Well'—recovering—'one mustn't be narrow-minded about these things. She's still a village woman, after all.'

Owen didn't quite follow.

'Well,' said Malik seriously. 'They all belong to me, you know. In principle. The whole village belongs to me.'

'I don't belong to you, you bastard,' muttered the barber, sotto voce.

'You mean, the women—?'

'Of course, I don't choose to exercise my rights. Not these days. But the right is still there. It's a matter of tradition. Tradition is very important to these people, you know, Owen. You wouldn't understand that, as an Englishman coming in from outside. But I know how important it is to them. They really *want* me to sleep with their wives. They expect it of me. And I, well, I really hate turning them down. It goes against the grain, Owen. But then I am also a man of the modern world. The fact is, I am torn. Torn, like all Egyptians, between the Old and the New.'

'Gosh, how difficult for you! And so you have to compromise? Instead of sleeping with all the women, you just sleep with the one who doesn't have a husband?'

'That's it! Exactly! Of course, I know that many will be disappointed, but—'

'I understand. But, my dear Malik, let me not add to the numbers of the disappointed by detaining you when you have pressing duties elsewhere—'

The car disappeared round the corner. The men circled round the chair watched it go.

'He thinks he owns us,' said someone bitterly.

'There'll come a time when all those Pashas are swept away,' said the barber.

'Not them! They'll hang on somehow or other. First, they'll sell themselves to the foreigners. Then they'll sell us.'

Owen, however, was wondering about his tidy separation of the village from the city.

⌘

As he was walking back to the station, Owen saw a woman working in the fields. She straightened up as he went past.

'It's no good, Effendi,' she said. 'Whatever you do, it is not going to bring him back.'

He stopped, surprised at being spoken to, although he knew that the women in the villages were much freer than those in the town. He guessed at once, though, who she was.

'You must be Leila,' he said. 'Ibrahim's wife.'

She nodded.

'I saw you,' she said, 'when you were talking to my father-in-law. And then you came again. You keep coming, don't you?'

'I keep coming,' Owen said. 'But really it is my colleague's concern, not mine.'

'Still you come, though. Well, I will tell my children and they will not forget. They are only daughters but they will tell their sons.'

'Thank you.' Owen looked around. 'They are not with you?'

'They are too small. Later—soon—they will come. When the man dies, the women have to work.'

'It is hard when the man goes.'

'And when he leaves no sons. We had hoped for sons but after Mariam's birth—well, I had a hard time that time and afterwards things were never quite the same. I was not right inside. Ibrahim paid for me to go to the *hakim* but he could do nothing. That is why,' she said, looking him in the face, 'he went to Jalila.'

Owen muttered something.

'It does not matter. Except that it angered my brothers. You have put my brothers in the *caracol*,' she said, not in accusation but as a matter of fact.

'Yes. Lest Ibrahim's family kill them in anger.'

'I do not think they would kill them. My brothers are strong men, stronger than they.'

'It is not that. It is that one has to stop the killing. One killing leads to another. One has to break the chain.'

'Perhaps,' she said.

'It is the first step that is wrong.'

'Yes, but what is the first step? The killing or what led to it?'

'Both are wrong. But when wrong is done, there are better remedies than killing.'

'Well, maybe.'

'*Did* your brothers look for revenge?'

'They looked.'

'But did they take it?'

She gave no sign of having heard. Instead, she said, almost wistfully:

'He was not a bad man. Foolish, yes, but not bad. His head was too hot and his tongue was too quick.'

'Was it too quick for your brothers?'

'For them?' She seemed startled. 'No. I do not think so. Ibrahim and Ali were friends,' she added, after a moment.

'Friends?' said Owen, surprised.

'Yes. That was how I came to wed. They met at the ostrich farm.'

'When Ibrahim was working there?'

'Ali worked there too. But only for a short time. He had worked for Zaghlul before, when Zaghlul was supplying the pilgrims. He used to manage the mules. But then when Zaghlul stopped, there was no work for him. Zaghlul offered him a job at the ostrich farm but Ali did not like it. He said, "This is no work for a man like me." "Very well, then," said Zaghlul, "you find your own work." Then Ali worked in the fields, but he did not like that either. He was always going off to the city. We would have spoken to him about it but he usually brought back money. Good money,' she said, considering.

'So he no longer works in the fields?'

'Oh, he does sometimes. At harvest time, of course. But also other times. And he still brings back money.'

'It was before he went to the city, then, that he was friends with Ibrahim?'

'No, they stayed friends after he'd left the ostrich farm. Ibrahim sometimes used to go with him into the city.'

'To the races?'

She looked at him in surprise.

'That is where Ali goes, isn't it?'

'Yes, but that is not where they went. They used to go to meetings.'

'Meetings?'

'Yes, big ones. Once,' she said with pride, 'they went to hear Mustapha Kamil.'

In a way it was no surprise. Thousands had gone to hear Mustapha Kamil, the charismatic young leader of the Nationalist Party, before he had died suddenly at a tragically early age. All the same, Owen hadn't expected it. Ali, the tough nut, the one who, if Mahmoud was right, consorted with racetrack gangs, and Ibrahim, the humble villager, going to political meetings?

And Nationalist ones? Well, they wouldn't have gone to any other, that was for sure. Politics was not for the likes of Ibrahim and Ali. Even the Nationalists drew their strength from office workers and the professional classes. They recognized that themselves. That, in a way, had been the point of the meeting that Owen had attended down by the Pont de Limoun. They had been trying to draw up support from the railway workers, without a lot of success.

But now here were two ordinary fellahs from the sticks turning up to listen to Mustapha Kamil! Unlikely ones, too, not exactly the sort you would see as avid readers of the Nationalist press, not the sort, actually, who could probably read at all. What was going on?

'Mustapha Kamil!' he said. 'There was a man!'

'There was a man indeed!' agreed Leila proudly.

'And Ali talked to you all about such things?'

'Oh, yes.'

He had underestimated Ali, only too evidently. He had seen only the rough, hard villager. What was it that she had said? Head too hot and tongue too quick?

But she had said that about Ibrahim, not about Ali.

'And Ibrahim, too, did he used to talk to you about such things?'

'At first, yes, but then his father would not let him. He said such talk was bad, that the Pasha would hear of it and be down on us. I think Fazal would have talked.'

'Fazal?'

'Ibrahim's brother.'

The difficult one. The one that Owen had thought might have looked for revenge for his brother's killing.

He still didn't think he was wrong. Only he had seen it all too simply. He had seen just the enmity, just the possible revenge relationship. He had not seen the relationships between the families. But relationships there were, of which the marriage between Leila and Ibrahim had been just one.

'And were they all still going to such meetings, Ali and Ibrahim?'

She was silent. Then she said:

'Mustapha Kamil is dead.'

'But there are others. Others now speak in his place.'

'There has been no time for meetings,' she said, 'not since Ibrahim began working for the Belgians.'

'They did not meet?'

'Only occasionally. Sometimes they would walk back to the village together.'

Suddenly she seemed to be far away. Perhaps she was remembering the past. Perhaps it was the first time since Ibrahim's death that she had allowed herself to.

'He was a good man,' Owen prompted gently.

'Yes.'

'But a hot-headed one, you said?'

'Yes.'

She laughed, remembering.

'And too quick of tongue. How was he too quick of tongue?'

'That time when he spoke up for the railwaymen. They were angry but no one would speak. Ibrahim was angry, too, but he said he would speak. His father wanted to beat him when he heard. Ali, too,' she said, surprisingly.

'Ali wanted to beat him?'

'Not beat him. But he said it was foolish to step forward. "Let others do that," he said.'

'Why did he say that?'

'He said it would do Ibrahim no good if he were to let himself be singled out. The job was not forever. Put up with it, he said, take the money, and then speak if you must.'

Owen was again surprised. Ali, the moderate? The man who had run for his gun that day?

'But Ibrahim did not take his advice,' he said.

'No.'

'Was Ali angry?'

'No. He said it was on his own head. But afterwards he came to him again and said: "There are men better at this than you." "Let them come forward, then," said Ibrahim. Well, Ali knew a man who wanted to work on the railway line and who was good at speaking and they let him come forward instead.'

'Was his name Wahid?' asked Owen.

As Owen approached the station he saw that a train was in. It was coming from Cairo, however, and no use to him. He was surprised, though, to see Mahmoud getting off.

Mahmoud, too, was disconcerted. He hesitated, gave Owen a slight bow with his head, and hurried past.

Owen was annoyed. Surely they had been friends for too long to mess about like this? On an impulse he turned and hurried after Mahmoud. Mahmoud heard the footsteps and looked round guardedly.

'Are you going to the village? I have just come from there. I picked up one or two things—perhaps I could discuss them with you?'

Mahmoud instantly warmed. Quick to perceive a slight, especially when it came from the British, he was also quick to respond to a sympathetic initiative. In fact, he tended to over-respond, especially when it came from Owen.

'I will stop. Where I was going does not matter. No, it does not matter at all. You are going back to Cairo? I will come with you!'

'No, no!' protested Owen. 'I will walk a little of the way with you. You were going to the village?'

'To the Tree. But I cannot allow you—'

After some while it was agreed that it was easier for Owen to accompany Mahmoud rather than vice versa and they set out across the fields. Owen looked to see if Leila was still there but she was not.

He was relieved to find that Mahmoud was still taking an interest in the village end of things. It had seemed that his attention was entirely on the railway and Owen felt that was unlikely to be productive.

He told Mahmoud what he had learned from his conversation with Leila. He hesitated for a moment over whether to tell him about the Nationalist meetings, but then decided that he would.

'So you see,' he said, 'there is this connection between Ibrahim and Ali.'

'The fact that they were friends,' said Mahmoud, thinking, 'wouldn't stop the brothers from exacting revenge. Revenge overrides everything in the Arab code of honour.'

'All the same—'

'Yes,' said Mahmoud, 'I am glad you told me.'

'And then there is the bit about the dispute, you know, the one on the railway that you are interested in, when Ibrahim acted as spokesman. I had been wondering why Ibrahim had acted as spokesman and not Wahid.'

'I made too much of that,' muttered Mahmoud.

'Well, I've probably been making too much of Wahid.'

'You were right, though. About the Nationalist connection.'

'But how important is it? So Wahid is a Nationalist. So are half a million other Egyptians.'

The mutual concessions restored their old relationship and by the time they reached the village they were talking happily.

'But you were going on to the Tree?'

'Well, yes. I wanted to see the place without so many people there.'

'I'm afraid—' began Owen guiltily.

But then Mahmoud saw the Tree with its guarding legions.

'What—?'

Owen explained.

'And they are guarding the Tree against the French?' said Mahmoud, amazed.

'And each other, yes.'

The guarding cohorts seemed for the time being, however, to have struck up an amicable alliance. They had found a brazier from somewhere and fuelled it with dried dung from around the well. The bitter fumes drifted across towards them. Daniel, the Copt, emerged from the balsam trees leading a donkey.

'Well, I'm off now,' he said, perching himself on the back of his donkey. 'Otherwise I won't get home in the light. There may be bad men about. Keep your eyes open!' he said to the Copts. 'I'll be back in the morning.'

'Don't worry,' said the Copts. 'It will still be here.'

They watched him go.

'Mean bastard,' they said. 'You'd think he'd have found us a chicken or two!'

'Isa's a mean bastard, too,' said one of the Sons of Islam. 'I reckon he's forgotten about us entirely.'

'The government's mean bastard, too,' said the policeman, looking at Owen.

'All right,' said Owen, 'I'll get somebody from the village to bring you up something.'

The men settled down around the brazier.

Mahmoud shrugged, then turned and walked a little way away and began looking round him. Owen knew he was trying to visualize what had happened.

But it had happened at night, thought Owen. There had been nothing to see. There had only been sounds in the darkness.

Over in the balsam trees around the well there was a little scurry and two goats came bounding out. Owen went across and found the old goatherd lying under a tree.

'Still here, then?'

'We've been over to Tel-el-Hasan for a couple of days,' said the old man. 'We'd have stayed longer but somebody had been there before us.'

'Eaten all the food, had they?'

'They've taken the lowest shoots. We can do better here.'

Owen sat down beside him. The heat had gone out of the sun now and the shadows were creeping over the sand.

'Tel-el-Hasan? Not many people go between there and here, do they?'

'Only the Copt.'

'You remember the night the man was found on the railway line?'

The old man nodded.

'And you heard voices up here by the Tree?'

'Yes.'

'Earlier that night, perhaps just when it was getting dark, did you see anyone coming over here from Tel-el-Hasan?'

The old man shook his head.

'A man, perhaps, or two men?'

'I saw no one.'

'Or even,' Owen persisted, 'a man and a woman? You said you had heard a man and a woman talking up by the Tree.'

'I heard. I did not see.'

'But earlier?'

The old man considered.

'I remember seeing no one,' he said finally.

Owen nodded. Mahmoud had probably already asked the questions.

'The goats were restless,' said the old man. 'It was a bad night.'

Owen made sympathetic noises. Up by the Tree, Mahmoud had walked off at a tangent and now was looking back at the spot where, according to the tracker, the attack had taken place. Owen guessed he was trying to work out how the two, the man and the woman, had approached. They must have been waiting by the Tree. But why had Ibrahim gone there anyway?

'It was a bad night,' said the old man again. 'The goats were restless. There was no quieting them down. First, the people. Then the bird.'

'Bird?' said Owen.

'There was a bird about. An ostrich.'

'You saw it?'

'No. But the goats knew. That was why they were restless.'

'When was this? About the time that you heard the people talking?'

'No. After.'

Puzzled, Owen went to join Mahmoud.

It was getting dark now and if they did not leave soon they might find it difficult to trace their way back across the fields to the station.

As they left the village behind they saw a long line of people coming across the desert. They were leading donkeys and camels heaped high with packs and some of them were carrying banners.

Owen and Mahmoud stopped to watch them pass.

'Have you thought,' said Mahmoud, 'that the concentration of pilgrims will be at its highest at just the moment that the new railway reaches Heliopolis?'

Chapter 10

Owen had not; but other people, it soon appeared, had. One of the Mamur Zapt's duties was to read the press for material of a politically inflammatory nature. Splashed across the front page of one of the most popular Nationalist newspapers the following morning was a heavy-breathing article drawing attention to the fact and making much of the insensitivity of the government and of foreign businessmen in allowing such a thing to happen. 'Surely,' the article concluded, 'someone could have foreseen how greatly traditional religious susceptibilities would be offended by such an untimely intrusion at an important moment of spiritual preparation.'

Owen had just put the newspaper down when the phone rang. It was the Syndicate.

'Have you seen—?'

'Yes, yes,' said Owen wearily.

'We wouldn't want everything to go wrong now. Not when we're so close to completion.'

'*Are* you so close to completion?'

'Another couple of weeks. Working Fridays will make all the difference.'

The railwaymen had in the end decided not to strike. They were too near the end of their contracts to want to lose money.

The railway, then, would be finished on time; and that would certainly be while the pilgrims were still congregated at Birket-el-Hadj. It took them several weeks to gather, not as long as in the past, when the first pilgrims would arrive months before departure, but long enough for them to be a considerable presence in the neighbourhood for some time.

But how close would the terminus of the railway actually be to Birket-el-Hadj?

'Not very close,' said the man from the Syndicate. 'We're ending it in Heliopolis. Quite near to the racecourse, as it happens.'

But distance, like so many other things, was blurred by the paper's feverish prose, and the next day another article appeared recording, with satisfaction, the volume of protest the paper had received about the foreigners' determination to press ahead and calling for a public demonstration at the Pont de Limoun the following evening.

The demonstration, coincidentally, was timed to start at exactly the moment that Mr Rabbiki, the veteran Nationalist politician, was due to initiate debate in the Assembly on the question he had put. The question, of course, was to do with Ibrahim and not with the arrival of the railway at Heliopolis, but Owen had no doubt that Mr Rabbiki's broad brush would tar widely.

'Any problems?' he asked Paul.

'Nothing that we can't handle,' said Paul confidently, 'if you can handle it at your end.'

Owen's end was the demonstration. It was far larger than the previous one. The Nationalist Party had pulled out all the stops and there were banners everywhere, a properly constructed platform for speakers, speakers of stature and a bodyguard of even greater stature to protect them, together with cohorts of supporters marched in for the occasion.

Owen, too, had pulled out all the stops and had policemen at all street corners and lots more policemen close at hand but tucked away discreetly out of sight.

He had stationed himself on the roof of one of the houses, from where he soon saw first that the number of demonstrators was greater than he had anticipated and then that the policemen he had left on the street corners had noticed this and prudently withdrawn into the cafés with their fellows.

The square below was full of people, their faces ruddy in the light of the torches that many of them held. They were listening quietly and attentively. Owen was always impressed by this, more impressed than he usually was by what was served out to them. They had a kind of hunger, the same hunger that Ali and Ibrahim had shown.

And patience, too, the long patience of the Egyptian fellahin, patience enough to listen for hours to the inflated rhetoric, the got-up emotion, about issues that were in the end unreal. What did they care about when the new railway would get to Heliopolis? What, for that matter, did the Nationalists care, either? The whole thing was being stage-managed just in order to create difficulty for the government.

But perhaps, thought Owen, listening with half an ear as the speeches entered their third hour, that was where the real issue came in. For what the political manoeuvring was ultimately about was who was going to govern Egypt. Who was going to do the stage-managing—Mr Rabbiki with his doomed question or Paul, behind the scenes, getting the Khedive and his Ministers to act to a script that was written in London?

But, hello, what was this? Something was going wrong with the script, or at least with his part of it! Over at the back of the crowd, in one corner, something was going on. The crowd was swirling around, breaking apart. Fighting? Was that fighting? He trained his field glasses.

Yes, fighting. He could see the clubs and sticks. But not among themselves. Someone was coming in from outside. It looked as if a great wedge had suddenly been driven into the back of the crowd. Surely his men had not come out without orders?

He'd have their blood for this! He turned and made for the outside steps leading down from the roof.

But wait! It wasn't them. They weren't in uniform. Who the hell were they? What the hell was going on?

⟨·ↄ⟩

Owen had his runners at the bottom of the steps, waiting for instructions. Each one knew the café where he had to go. They went at once. Within minutes, policemen were pouring out of the café.

The Cairo constables were for the most part country boys, chosen for their size and strength and, some alleged, their simplicity. Given orders to clear a square, they would.

They had, moreover, the advantage of surprise. The crowd, confused already by the disturbance at the rear, split apart under their charge and the separate parts were forced back upon the exits from the square. Many of the torches fell down or were extinguished and in the darkness it was hard to see anything. There was only the pressure of bodies driving people to the edges of the square, the confused shouting and screaming and the incessant blast of the police whistles.

There was hardly any resistance. The crowd was largely unarmed. There were the usual few with knives and clubs but, hemmed in by people and in the darkness, they were unable to use them.

Only in one part of the square, where the original wedge had burst into the crowd, was there serious fighting. The men there were armed and were holding the constables back.

Owen gathered a few extra men and ran across. There were no torches here, but in the dim light from a nearby café he could see a struggling throng of men.

'Police!' he shouted. 'Back!'

There was a moment's uncertainty and then men detached themselves from the throng and came back towards him.

'Form into line!' he shouted.

The men spread out on both sides of him. For a moment they stood breathing heavily and looking at the dark mass of men ahead of them.

'Line: Advance!'

The line moved forward. This was the moment when training and discipline told. Or so Owen hoped.

Someone pushed up beside him.

'You might need this.'

He recognized the voice. It was one of his plainclothesmen, a Greek.

He felt a gun being pushed into his hand.

Suddenly, things were different.

'Line: Halt!' he shouted. And then, in a moment of inspiration: 'Prepare to fire!'

The constables halted, obedient but confused. Batons were all they had.

'This is the Mamur Zapt,' he called out to the dark mass in front of him. 'I order you to disperse! If you do not, I shall open fire. I shall fire one shot into the air to show you that I am armed.'

The sharp crack came almost at once.

There was a sudden silence in the square.

'Disperse immediately! Or I shall open fire.'

He would, too.

But there was no need. The dark line ahead of him wavered and broke. In an instant men were running.

The constables moved in. A man came reeling back, dazed and nursing an arm. Owen caught him by the galabeah and then, as that would tear, by the hair.

The square was emptying rapidly now, as the crowd fled in panic.

⌘

'Not good, though,' said Owen, as he sat in the bar of the Sporting Club at lunchtime the next day.

'Not good at all,' Paul agreed. 'It's given Mr Rabbiki his publicity triumph on a plate.'

The veteran politician had not waited long to capitalize on the disaster. Early the next morning he had appeared in Owen's office, stern but undisguisedly cheerful.

'An outrage!' he said. 'We demand a public apology.'

'You can have one from me,' said Owen. 'I'm damned annoyed at what happened.'

'Oh, we don't want one from you,' said Mr Rabbiki. 'We want one from the government.'

'You'll be lucky!'

'Well, it doesn't really matter,' said Mr Rabbiki, catching the smell of coffee—all meetings in Cairo, whether adversarial or convivial, required coffee—and relaxing, 'since we've got what we wanted.'

'All went according to plan, did it?' said Owen sourly.

Rabbiki gave him a quick look.

'No,' he said, 'it did not. We had planned a straightforward demonstration. Large, but peaceful. What happened? Who were those men?'

'I don't know,' said Owen, 'but I'm damned well going to find out!'

'They weren't police, I know that.'

'No, I sent the police in afterwards. Once the fighting had started. I wanted to break it all up before it had a chance of spreading.'

'You took a risk,' said Mr Rabbiki accusingly. 'With all those people, someone might have got killed.'

'I know that. That's why I'm so annoyed.'

'I can tell you who the men were,' said Mr Rabbiki. 'They were Syndicate men.'

'I doubt that. What would be the point?'

'They know we want to stop the railway from getting to Heliopolis on time. This was intended as a warning.'

'If it was,' said Owen, 'then it was a very stupid one.'

'We are dealing with some very stupid people.'

'Are we? I'm not so sure about that.'

'Nor am I, on second thoughts,' Mr Rabbiki admitted. 'Stupid, possibly. Ruthless, certainly.'

'Well—'

'As they have shown in the case of that poor man whose body was found on the railway line. I hope, Captain Owen, that while you're grappling with these wider political issues, you won't lose sight of what happened to that poor man.'

'If I did, Mr Rabbiki,' said Owen, smiling, 'I'm sure you would put down a question. Coffee?'

ᐤᵐᵐᵒ

'But was it wise?' asked the man from the Syndicate, half an hour or so after Mr Rabbiki had gone.

'Wise?'

'To break up the demonstration so, well, firmly? I know we've asked you to take a strong line but, well, frankly, we'd prefer a little more finesse just at the moment, with the line so near completion. Only another couple of weeks to go! You don't think you could lie low for that period, do you? We really do appreciate your efforts on our behalf, believe me, we know you're doing your best, but—you couldn't handle things with a bit more sensitivity, could you?'

ᐤᵐᵐᵒ

'Sensitivity!' he said to Paul indignantly. 'Those bastards! Me!'

'They were just having fun,' said Paul confidently. 'Trying to provoke you!'

'No, they weren't. They meant it!'

'Really?'

'Yes, really. That was the message: hold back! Show a bit more sensitivity! Let's have a bit more finesse! Those brutal sods!'

'Well,' said Paul, reflecting, 'I suppose they think they've almost got there. Brutality is what you need on the way; sensitivity and finesse is what it's called once you've got there.'

He signalled to the waiter for another drink.

'But why,' he said, 'would they have taken that line if all the time they were behind it?'

'To cover up,' said Owen.

'You think they were just trying to put you off?'

'I don't know,' said Owen, 'but I'm going to find out. And when I do, I'll show them some bloody sensitivity!'

ᐤᵐᵐᵒ

Most shops in Cairo closed for the afternoon. Most police stations did, too, their inhabitants arguing, reasonably, that if it was too hot for work it was also too hot for crime. Not, however, the police headquarters at the Bab-el-Khalk, where Owen had his office. Some men had been arrested the night before at the demonstration and lodged in the local police station. This morning they had been transferred up, and now Owen meant to interview them himself.

The first three, however, were ordinary members of the crowd. Not entirely ordinary citizens, perhaps, since they had all been armed and had attempted to use their weapons against the constables, which accounted first for their battered appearance and then for their arrest. Owen, though, was not interested in them. What he wanted was someone from the invading wedge. He remembered the man he had himself arrested and went down to the cells to find him.

On the way back to his room they passed Garvin, the Commandant, who cast a professional eye over the prisoners.

'Oh, Abbas,' he said, 'it's you, is it?'

'I wasn't doing anything this time, Effendi,' protested the man indignantly.

'Got arrested by accident? Well, blow me!'

'What were you doing near the Pont de Limoun, then?' asked Owen, when he had got the man settled in his room.

'Nothing!'

Owen pointed to the man's arm, which was in a rough sort of sling.

'How come you got hit on the arm, then?'

'The fact is, Effendi, I wasn't looking. At least, not on that side, I'd got this bloke lined up, a big, fat policeman he was, and I thought, Right, my beauty, I'll have you! And then, damn me, someone comes at me from the side and catches me a crack, I thought it had broke my arm, and then before I could do anything about it, the other one turns round and gives me a crack over the head! I tell you, in future I'm always going to make sure I'm paired up with someone, it's better that way, one of you can keep a lookout while the other's doing the hitting. Then you can take turn and turn about. Hosayn's the man, I think, he's quite quick and not stupid—'

He had an attitude to the fighting that was purely technical and Owen soon put him down as a professional heavy, a member of a gang most likely, brought in for occasions.

Had he been brought in on this occasion?

Certainly, the man replied with pride. Word had gone round that good men were required and he and several others had put their names forward. They had worked with Figi before—

Figi?

'He's our boss. We don't work with him all the time, but lately he's been getting some good contracts—'

Like?

'Well, this one. Go in and break them up. Very straight-forward. And they probably wouldn't even be armed! Well, I mean—'

And that was all?

Well, it was enough, wasn't it? The reward had to be matched against the risk, after all. In this case there hadn't seemed to be much risk so they'd settled for something quite low. And then the Mamur Zapt had come along and started shooting!

'You never know,' said the man philosophically.

And, indeed, he didn't know. Not much more than he'd said, anyway. Owen got more out of Garvin, into whose office he dropped after the man had been taken away.

'Oh, yes,' said Garvin, 'I know him. He works the racetracks. Stays with the same gang, mostly.'

'Do they take on other jobs?'

'Occasionally.'

'Political ones?'

Garvin looked doubtful.

'I wouldn't have thought so. Mostly they stick to the race-tracks...They were up at Heliopolis the other day,' he offered as Owen was on the way out.

Owen stopped.

'The ones we saw?'

'That's right. They were talking to one of the stewards, if you remember. I'm worried about that, Owen. We don't want the course to get off to a bad start. You asked me not to take action, but—'

⁂

'Hello!' said Salah-el-Din, coming across the room to greet him. 'What brings you here?'

'I was over at Matariya,' said Owen, 'so I thought I would pop in.'

'Very nice to see you. Care for a drink?'

This being Cairo, Owen didn't ordinarily accept drinks from subordinates; but this was also the bar at the New Heliopolis Racing Club, where things certainly seemed a bit different, so he accepted graciously.

They sat down in two plushy armchairs near the window, from where they could look down on the racetrack. There being no races today, the track was empty; except for, yes, it was her, Salah-el-Din's daughter, plus attendant, going for her usual promenade.

Salah-el-Din followed the direction of Owen's eyes.

'Yes, it is Amina. We come most days. But she goes for a walk while I come up to the bar!' He laughed. 'In case you're wondering, though, I only have one drink. And I justify my attendance on the grounds that until more of Heliopolis is built, this is where I'm going to meet everybody.'

The bar was certainly filling up. There was a sprinkling of Syndicate staff, mostly Belgians but a number of—well, not so much effendis, too rich for that—wealthy Egyptian young, all males, of course, from the Pashas' houses round about. Owen looked for Malik. He wasn't there, but if Amina was, could Malik be far behind?

They talked for a while about the new police station that was being built at Heliopolis and about its staffing. This was really Garvin's pigeon but Salah was anxious that there should be some Mamur Zapt involvement, on the grounds that the international community, bankers and such, would be heavily represented in the New Heliopolis and policing would have to have regard for international treaties.

Owen offered a return drink, which, however, Salah declined.

'Since I've told you my role, I'd better stick to it,' he said. 'However, you can offer it to Amina if you like. I'm just going down to fetch her.'

'I'll come with you, if I may,' said Owen. 'I'd like to look at the track.'

Some men were laying turf.

'Big staff?'

'Building up,' said Salah. 'People don't realize how many the Club will employ. It will be a very good thing for people hereabouts.'

'And for the gangs.'

'I've seen that here already. That's one of the things I'm going to have to keep an eye on.'

'Do they get at the staff? Try to influence them?'

'It wouldn't do any good. You've got to have safeguards against a thing like that.'

Owen looked for the man he had seen the other day.

'What happens to the stewards? Are they here all the time?'

'Just for the races.'

There would be races the following Saturday, Salah said. The Club was anxious to hold them twice a week but at the moment the crowds didn't justify it.

'It'll be different when the new railway's running,' he said.

Amina's eyes, above her veil, brightened when she saw Owen.

'You've still not been to see me,' she said accusingly. 'I ride every morning, mostly over towards Matariya.'

'I've been a bit busy lately. One of these mornings you'll see me!'

The horse would have to be wild indeed that got him over to Matariya, he told himself privately.

'About seven,' she said.

'Lot of people around at that time?' he said, wondering about Malik.

'Fortunately not,' she said, meeting his eyes levelly.

Up in the bar, he bought her a drink. She chose tonic.

She was the only woman in the room. Owen noticed, however, that they seemed to accept her. Probably they'd got used to her. It wouldn't do, though, to talk to her all the time. Or would it? This was a different world from any other that he had known in Egypt, not exactly more emancipated, but freer in the way that wealth somehow manages to give itself more elbow room.

Salah brought someone across to meet him.

'George Zenakis,' he said. 'Our Secretary.'

Our Secretary?

'You must be very busy just now,' said Owen, 'with everything starting up.'

'Well, yes. But it's nothing to what it's going to be later. Or so they tell me,' the man said, smiling.

'And do you handle everything? Or is there a General Manager of some sort?'

'I handle everything on behalf of the committee. Membership, for instance.'

'How many members have you?'

'About two hundred, and growing fast. You wouldn't yourself—?'

'I'm afraid I wouldn't be able to get out here enough. My other commitments—'

He asked, for politeness's sake, about the subscription, then mentally reeled back.

'I don't think I could run to that,' he said.

'Oh, you don't have to bother about that,' said George Zenakis, smiling. 'We would be glad to waive, for the Mamur Zapt—'

☙

On the Saturday, Owen was at the races. Not up in the bar this time but down by the track, and not there for long; just long enough to point out to his agents the steward that he and Garvin had seen talking to the gang on the day of the reception.

'His name is Roukoz,' said Georgiades in Owen's office on the following Monday. Georgiades was the plain-clothesman who had put a gun into Owen's hand at the demonstration. 'And he has a history of working the racetracks. He was at the Gezira for a little while but they didn't like him and so he moved on to Helwan.'

'Why didn't they like him?' asked Owen.

'He was too friendly with the wrong sort of people.'

'The gang?'

'Gangs. Nothing they could put their finger on, but they didn't like him.'

'And at Helwan?'

Georgiades hesitated.

'Nothing you could put your finger on there, either. But again they didn't like him. This time, though, he had a friend higher up and so he stayed.'

'Do you know the friend?'

'Yes. He's not at Helwan either now.'

'Where is he?'

'Heliopolis.'

'Who moved first?'

'The friend did. Then, when the racetrack opened, Roukoz.'

'What's the name of the friend?'

'Zenakis.'

༄

Owen went to see the man from the Syndicate who had rung him up.

'About that demonstration the other night,' he said. 'I didn't break it up.'

'You didn't? But—who did?'

'You did,' said Owen.

'Now look here, Owen—'

'You used a gang from the racetracks. I know. I've got one of them.'

'If you say it was a gang from the racetracks, OK, it was a gang from the racetracks. But it wasn't anything to do with us.'

'Well, I think it was. I know the gang, you see, and I've seen them at Heliopolis.'

'Yes, but that doesn't mean—'

'Talking to one of the stewards.'

'That's bad. It must be looked into. But that doesn't necessarily—'

'He's a friend of the Club Secretary. A close friend.'

'Zenakis?'

'That's right.'

'I know Zenakis.'

'That's what I'm saying.'

There was a long silence.

'Look, Owen—'

'If you're going to ask me to handle this with sensitivity, you'll have to try again.'

'I wasn't going to—Look, you've got this all wrong.'

'So have you. So,' said Owen, 'have you!'

'I know you're sore. I shouldn't have said what I did the other morning. OK, I've got it wrong. But you've got it wrong too.'

'Oh yes?'

'Yes. It wasn't your people who broke up the demonstration, I accept that. But'—he took a deep breath—'it wasn't ours either. I swear we don't know anything about it.'

'No?'

'If for no other reason than that it wouldn't be in our interest. We're nearly there, as I said the other morning. All we want to do is to wrap it up and get out. Besides—'

'Keep trying.'

'Zenakis is not the Syndicate. He's not ours. The Racing Club is quite separate. All that side is. All the gambling bit. They're clients of ours, customers. It's a separate organization. It's nothing to do with us. Honest!'

Chapter 11

There was racing the next day at Heliopolis and the gang turned up in force; so, in even greater force, did Owen's men, and arrested the lot of them.

'What's all this about?' they said in injured tones. 'We haven't done anything yet!'

'What about breaking up that demonstration on Wednesday?'

'That doesn't count!' they protested. 'That's not a real crime. People do it all the time. Besides, it was just an extra, not our real line of business at all.'

'We work the racetracks,' explained someone helpfully.

'Yes, I know,' said Owen.

'Who the hell are you, anyway?' said someone belligerently. 'You're not police, we know the police.'

'I am the Mamur Zapt.'

'What's it got to do with you?'

'Abdul, don't you think you could shut up?' counselled one of the older members of the gang worriedly. 'If he's the Mamur Zapt, he might do things differently from the police.'

He certainly might. One of his predecessors, Zeini Barakat, infuriated by just such a gang, had ordered their testicles to be cut off and fed to the hawks that hovered above the Citadel. That had, admittedly, been four hundred years before, but you never knew with Mamur Zapts and the gang was impressed.

'You don't want to bother with us, Effendi,' they said conciliatorily. 'We're just a small-time gang.'

'It's true I don't want to bother with you,' agreed Owen. 'I've got more important things to do. And therefore I shall release you. Once you've told me what I want to know.'

'What do you want to know, Effendi?'

'Who asked you to break up the demonstration.'

The gang consulted among themselves.

'It came through our boss.'

'Figi?'

'Well—'

'Is Figi here?'

Figi, as is the way with bosses when there is trouble around, was not.

'No matter. Let Figi know what I want. And meanwhile you stay here.'

No need to inquire too closely into how they would contact Figi. They would probably bribe a prison official. But the message would get through.

'Stay here? But, Effendi, if we stay here we won't be able to do any work.'

'That's exactly what I was thinking,' said Owen.

The point evidently occurred to Figi, too, for that afternoon a message came up from the cells that the gang wished to speak to Owen.

'Well?'

'Effendi, it's not fair. While we're in the *caracol* we can't do any work and Figi doesn't get any money.'

'True,' said Owen.

'He wishes to protest.'

'All he has to do is give me the name.'

'He has sent the name. But he wishes to protest.'

'I note the protest. What is the name?'

'Roukoz. He works at Heliopolis and—'

'I know the man,' said Owen.

'Roukoz,' said Owen, 'here is a bad thing that I have heard: friends tell me that it was you who ordered the attack on the demonstration on Wednesday.'

'Effendi, your friends lie! Would I do a thing like that? A humble, hard-working, peace-loving father of six? Those who say that are villains!'

'Would you like to tell them so?'

'Effendi, outraged by calumny and injustice, I would!'

'They await you in the *caracol*.'

'On second thoughts, Effendi—'

'Who told you to contact the gang?'

'Effendi, I know no gang.'

'You have never spoken to them?'

'Never!'

'Not the other day at Heliopolis? The day of the grand reception?'

'Certainly not!'

'Well, that is strange. For I saw you speak to them myself. And so did the Chief of all the Police.'

Roukoz swallowed.

'It is easy to make a mistake, Effendi—'

'So it is,' Owen agreed. 'And that's exactly what you have done. Now tell me: who told you to get the gang to break up the demonstration?'

Zenakis advanced across the room with outstretched hand.

'The Mamur Zapt again? What a pleasure!'

'It is indeed!' agreed Owen. 'Shall we go into your office?'

Zenakis, once he had taken the measure of the situation, did not seriously attempt to deny responsibility.

'This is Cairo, after all,' he said with a shrug of his shoulders. 'Completion of the railway is important to us. And the Nationalist campaign was gathering momentum.'

'You leave the Nationalists to me!'

'Ordinarily we would. But we knew your hands were tied.'

'"We"?'

Zenakis hesitated.

'"I", I should have said.'

'You acted on your own responsibility?'

'Within the broad remit given me by the committee. But I take full responsibility for what happened the other night and if apologies are called for, I apologize.'

'How far did the committee know what you were doing?'

'They have given me, as I say, a broad remit.'

'Who is on the committee?'

Zenakis gave him several names.

'A strong committee,' Owen commented.

The list contained several Pashas and relatives of Pashas—Malik was there—and also two members of the Khedive's own family. Owen could see now why Zenakis appeared so confident.

'I take full responsibility,' said Zenakis. 'If error there was, it was mine. However, it was done with the best intentions. We felt you needed some help. Sometimes,' he said, eyes twinkling, 'one would be glad of help but is unable to ask for it.'

'If I need help,' said Owen, 'I'll ask for it!'

Inwardly, he fumed. There was nothing he could do. Zenakis had admitted responsibility and yet it would be difficult to take action against him. Breaking up a demonstration, in Cairo, was hardly a crime. Even Mahmoud would hesitate about initiating legal proceedings. And where would it get him? In the unlikely event of Zenakis being found guilty, he would be pardoned at once by the Khedive. And was Zenakis the man really responsible anyway? Wasn't he just covering up for the committee?

Zenakis took him by the arm.

'Now that's over, how about a drink? And have you thought again about membership?'

There was trouble at the Tree. So said Salah-el-Din's cryptic message. It also said that he would hold the fort until Owen got there. But he suggested that he hurry.

At the Tree, Owen found the rival camps bristling. The Copts, truculent, were drawn up on one side, ostentatiously examining their knives; the Sons of Islam, even more truculent, on the other, holding their daggers up to the setting sun and commenting loudly on the way in which it dyed their blades red. In the middle, not at all truculent, but distinctly apprehensive, were Owen's guards, presided over temporarily by the determined Salah-el-Din. On the outskirts of it all, for some reason that Owen could not fathom, was Salah-el-Din's daughter, Amina, sitting on a horse.

'What's all this about?' demanded Owen.

'He's going to sell the Tree,' said one of the Sons of Islam, pointing an accusing finger at Daniel, the Copt, skulking behind the other Copts.

'It's my property!' retorted Daniel. 'I can do with it as I like!'

'Selling your birthright!' jeered the Sons of Islam.

'It's not your property!' cried a loud voice from behind Owen. It was Sheikh Isa, hurrying up on his donkey.

'It *is* my property!' cried Daniel indignantly, emerging from behind the row of Copts and forgetting to skulk.

'Blackguard!' cried Sheikh Isa, swinging a bony leg over his donkey and descending to the ground.

'Villain!' cried Daniel, and rushed on him.

The Copt and Muslim lines moved forward.

Owen caught hold of Isa and Daniel and thrust them apart.

'What is all this nonsense?' he said. 'No one is selling the Tree!'

'Well…' said Daniel uncomfortably.

'Ha!' cried Sheikh Isa.

'Actually—' began Salah-el-Din.

Owen turned on him.

'Do you know anything about this?'

'The Syndicate has made him an offer.'

'Which I am considering,' said Daniel modestly.

'The bastard's accepted!' cried one of the Sons.

'It's not his to accept!' shouted Sheikh Isa.

'The question of ownership is in the hands of the courts,' said Owen. 'That's why you're here. Guarding the Tree until the question is resolved. Which won't be for years.'

'Why have they made him an offer, then?' asked Sheikh Isa.

Owen turned again to Salah.

'The offer is not, strictly speaking, for the Tree, but for any claims he may have for the Tree. The same offer has been made to the descendents of the Empress Eugenie and, indeed, to anyone else who has claims to the Tree—'

'It hasn't been made to me!' cried Sheikh Isa.

'Legally, you don't have—' began Salah.

'That's right!' Daniel interrupted gleefully. 'You don't even have a recognizable claim!'

'We're pretty recognizable!' said the Sons of Islam.

'The Khedive gave the Tree—' began Salah-el-Din.

'Gave?' said Isa incredulously. 'The Holy Tree? Something that is the property of Islam? It was not his to give. Who is this Khedive? I don't recognize *him*!'

'Death to the Khedive!' shouted the Sons of Islam.

'That's right!' cried the Copts joyfully. 'Death to the Khedive!'

The Sons glared at them.

'And to the Christians!'

'Who would give away the Tree!' interrupted Sheikh Isa.

'Sell it,' corrected Daniel. 'Not give it.'

'Never!' said Sheikh Isa. 'Over my dead body!'

'So be it!' said Daniel, signalling to the Copts.

'For Christ's sake!' said Owen. 'Get back, the lot of you! Guards!'

'Look out!' cried one of the Sons. 'He shot down the Faithful in the square the other night!'

'Shot down the Faithful?' said Sheikh Isa.

'Well done!' chorused the Copts.

Daniel and Isa threw themselves upon one another.

Owen wrestled them apart.

'Get him away!' he said to Salah over his shoulder.

Salah hustled Daniel off. Owen caught Sheikh Isa by the folds of his galabeah and heaved him out of earshot of the rival supports. 'Now you listen to me—'

'Now you listen to me,' he said to the assembled company a few minutes later. 'I have agreed with Sheikh Isa that until the courts have spoken, the Tree cannot be sold.'

Daniel opened his mouth.

'And have told him that if the Copt takes any action in the meantime I shall confiscate the property on behalf of the Khedive.'

'I don't think, actually, that you can—' began Salah uncomfortably.

Owen silenced him with a baleful look.

'And I myself will speak with those who would buy the Tree. It may be that they will change their mind. One thing is certain, though: and that is that if I have any more trouble from any of you—'

Copts and Sons listened to the tirade admiringly. Owen made it long to give them time to calm down; and made it funny to restore their good humour. At the end, they stood for a moment or two uncertainly and then sat down.

Daniel came up to Owen and plucked him by the sleeve.

'Effendi—'

'And you,' said Owen, 'go home.'

'Go home?' said Daniel astonished.

'That's right. Get on your donkey and go.'

Daniel hesitated, shrugged, then went down among the balsam trees and collected his donkey. They watched him climb on to its back and set off in the direction of Tel-el-Hasan.

'It's all right for him,' said one of the Sons to one of the Copts. 'You've got to stay here.'

'You know,' said the Copt, 'I think that every night when he gets on his donkey and sets off for his comfortable bed.'

'Comfortable wife, too, I wouldn't be surprised,' said the Son of Islam. He looked across at Sheikh Isa. 'It's all right for him, too. He just gets on his donkey and off he goes. We've got to stay here. And we've got wives, too!'

Camaraderie restored, the two sat down happily to grumble together.

'I will send up chickens for tonight,' said Owen. 'Or at least, Heliopolis will.'

He looked at Salah.

'Definitely!' promised Salah.

Owen had words for Salah, too.

'If the Syndicate goes behind my back just once again—'

'I was going to tell you,' said Salah hurriedly.

'What are they after? Trying to buy the Tree? It's nowhere near the line of the railway.'

'Malik wants to use the land for training gallops,' said a voice behind him.

He had forgotten about Amina.

'You were terrific,' she said.

'Thanks. What's it got to do with him?'

'The committee has hopes of a training stable. It would have to be on this side because they're building on the other ones. He's got an interest of his own, too. He has some land over here which he thinks could be part of it.'

'Just a minute, it's the Syndicate that's buying the land, isn't it? Not the committee.'

'The Syndicate's buying the land *for* the committee.'

Salah cut in quickly, with an annoyed look at his daughter.

'The Syndicate is developing the site. It builds the facilities and then lets them to clients like the Racing Committee.'

'Which keeps asking for more and more.'

'Amina!' said Salah angrily. 'It is time you went. Ride on!'

Amina gave Owen a smile as she went.

'Remember,' she said, 'I ride over this way every morning.'

'On your way, girl!' shouted Salah furiously. 'Sometimes I wonder,' he said to Owen, 'if I've brought her up in quite the right way!'

'Immodesty upon immodesty!' cried Sheikh Isa, who had only just seen Amina. 'Abomination upon abomination! A woman! On a horse!'

⟡

'My fortune is made!' called the barber as Owen passed. 'Come and rejoice at my wealth!'

Owen dropped into the little circle around the chair.

'How is your fortune made?'

'The Belgians wish to buy my land.'

'You haven't got any land,' one of the circle objected.

'My cousin has.'

'It's only an allotment. Which he shares with Musa.'

'Land is land. And it's right in the way of what Malik wants for his gallops. I shall hold out! Whatever he offers me, I shall spurn. "You offer me *that?*" I shall say, "I disdain your puny offer. You'll have to offer serious money if you want to get anywhere with me!"'

'But it's not your land!'

'It's my cousin's land. And my cousin is but a fool, a simple man. He has no head for this kind of thing. I shall negotiate for him.'

'Against the Pasha? He'll have your balls off!'

'Anyway,' said another of the circle, 'I thought you didn't agree with selling off the Tree to foreigners?'

'The Tree? What is the Tree? It is mere superstition. Sell it off, I say. Pocket the money. The money is real; the Tree is but vapour.'

'This is a different tune from what you were singing yesterday.'

'I sing with the times. I am,' said the barber with dignity, 'on the side of Progress.'

'Now you are, but—'

'You'll never make any money out of this!'

'Malik's the one who'll make the money.'

'Oh, I don't know about that,' said someone else. 'Zaghlul owns some of the land, too, and he's not going to sell. He doesn't like Malik.'

'He'll sell if the money's right.'

'No, he won't. Just to spite Malik.'

'Anyway,' said someone who had not yet spoken, 'what does Malik want a gallop for? He goes on enough gallops with Jalila!'

They all laughed.

'Not any more, he doesn't,' said the barber. 'She won't have anything to do with him now. Not since Ibrahim died.'

'Why not?' asked Owen.

'She used to like Ibrahim. Of course, she had to go with Malik if he asked her, because he was the Pasha. But she preferred Ibrahim. Anyway, one day when he called, there was Ibrahim. "Bugger off!" he says to Ibrahim. Well, you know Ibrahim. Head too hot, tongue too quick. "It's not for me to bugger off," he says. "Times have changed. You don't own me now. And it won't be long before you and your lot'll be swept away." "Oh, is that so?" says Malik. "We'll see about that!" And then, do you know, that stupid woman has to butt in. "Take yourself off!" she says to Malik. "He's right. You don't own him now and you don't own me either." So off Malik has to go, with his tail between his legs.'

'She oughtn't to have said that!' said someone. 'Not to the Pasha!'

'Well, she's sticking to it. He's been over to see her several times and each time she says, "Not you, Malik."'

'She was always too outspoken,' said someone uneasily.

လ၀ာ၀

Owen went to see Jalila.

'Well,' she said, 'this is a surprise!'

Her brother was obviously not there, for she did not invite him in.

'I'm still looking for the man who killed Ibrahim.'

'Yes,' she said, 'I know you are.' There was a pause and then she said: 'You've got him, haven't you?'

'Have I?'

She did not reply.

'What did you come to see me for?'

'Ibrahim and Malik quarrelled. Since then you have refused to see Malik. Why?'

'What's the Pasha's son to me?' she said. 'Ibrahim was right. Their day has gone.'

'Is that all?'

'What else could there be?'

'Did Malik come to see you on the night that Ibrahim was killed?'

She looked at him in surprise.

'No.'

'Sure?'

She suddenly understood.

'If Malik had been anywhere around,' she said bitterly, 'I would have told you.'

☙

He had felt he had to explore it. But really he could not see it. A quarrel over a woman, affronted pride, revenge taken, yes; but Malik? Somehow Owen could not see him in the part. Ali, now, Leila's ferocious brother, that was a different matter: a rough, tough customer, used, probably, to such work through his association with the racecourse gang, quick, as Owen had seen for himself, to reach for a gun in an argument, more than ready to resent an affront—Owen could certainly see him doing it.

And that, clearly, was what the village thought. Even Jalila herself, probably. Malik? He didn't come into it—except that he obviously loomed much larger in the life of the village than Owen had supposed.

Besides, one always came back to it—if Malik had been involved, what could one make of the body's being placed on the line? It was directly contrary to Malik's interests. What he wanted was to get the line completed as quickly as possible. No, revenge might have had some part to play in Ibrahim's death, but it wouldn't have been Malik's desire for revenge—if desire for revenge he had; more likely, he viewed the whole thing as simply beneath him—but someone else's. There seemed to be plenty of desire for revenge washing around the village, not least on the part of Ali. And that, Owen was convinced, was far more likely.

Coming out of Sheikh Isa's house he saw Zaghlul. Unexpectedly, the old man crossed the street and came up to him.

'This is a bad business,' he said.

'There are many bad businesses, especially just now. Which one is troubling you?'

Instead of replying, Zaghlul nodded his head.

'Yes,' he said, 'there are many bad businesses just now. But they all come from one thing. Two years ago everything here was like that.' He pointed out across the fields shimmering in the sun to the more distant shimmer of the desert. 'Now,' he said, 'it is like that.'

He gestured towards the houses.

'Everywhere they build. The city creeps out into the desert. The railway—'

He spat into the dust.

'They squeeze us out,' he said. 'At first we say: "The desert is big enough for both of us," and let them come. But the desert is not big enough for both of us. They want more and yet more. They squeeze us out.

'At first I said: "The times are changing and I must change with them." I saw the railway coming out to Heliopolis and saw them building the big stores. And I said to myself: "Zaghlul, you must learn new tricks." So I bought some land out in the desert, away from Heliopolis, and I stocked it with ostriches. And I thought, "Here I will be safe," for it is away from Heliopolis and among the palaces of the Khedives and the Pashas and they will not let them build there. But always they want more. Now they are building these gallops.'

'Not yet,' said Owen. 'And, anyway, does it matter? The gallops will be land, not houses. And they are still two miles from your farm.'

'But what if they want more gallops?' Zaghlul shook his head. 'Ostriches and horses don't get along with each other. They smell each other and and are frightened.'

'Zaghlul,' said Owen, remembering suddenly, 'are other animals besides horses frightened by ostriches? Goats, for instance?'

'Goats?' said Zaghlul, startled. 'I do not know. I have not thought about it.'

'I have heard that it is so. But if it were so, the bird would have to pass close, would it not?'

'It is the smell. They would have to be able to smell it.'

'But then, if it passed close, in the night, let us say, they would be disturbed and restless?'

'I would expect so.'

'Yes,' said Owen, 'I would expect so. Tell me, Zaghlul, do your birds often escape?'

'That is what they say,' said Zaghlul, 'but it is a lie!'

'There was one that escaped. I saw it.'

'There would have been no problem if that fool Malik had not chased it and scared it. I would have caught it and it would have been back behind the fences before anyone knew anything about it!'

'So they do escape?'

'Occasionally. But—'

'And you pursue them. Tell me, Zaghlul, did one escape on the night that Ibrahim was killed? And did you by any chance pursue it?'

Zaghlul's face darkened.

'You take the side of the city,' he said angrily. 'For you, my ostriches are always breaking out. No, one did not break out on the night that Ibrahim was killed. And no, I did not pursue it.'

He stumped furiously away and a little later Owen saw him riding off into the fields on his way back to his farm.

For a moment the village street was empty and then a group of women came along, chattering as they went to fetch water for the evening meal. They called out to Owen cheerfully as they passed. Everyone in the village knew him, he suddenly realized. He had been out here so often over the past two weeks that they almost took him for granted.

The first smells of the evening cooking drifted down the street. A particularly pungent whiff made him splutter. Someone must have just thrown a load of too-recently-dried cattle dung on to a fire.

Men were coming back from the fields with hoes and baskets and a donkey nodded past carrying a huge load of *berseem*. The doves in the palms around the well were beginning to take up their evening cooing, a low, fulfilled murmur which would go on until the sun dropped finally beneath the horizon.

Another of the sounds had changed, too. For a moment he did not realize what it was, and then he saw a man lifting the small boy down from the back of the ox that had driven the water-wheel.

The day's work in the village was coming to an end. Men would be walking back from the irrigation channels, the ostrich farm, the railway or wherever they worked. Everyone would be going home. Daniel, the Copt, would—on a normal day—be untethering his donkey in the grove of balsam trees and preparing to set out on the journey back to Tel-el-Hasan.

Owen stopped.

Daniel, the Copt, would, on a normal day, be just starting out on the journey back to Tel-el-Hasan.

Chapter 12

The following morning Owen was at the Tree again; not as early as Daniel, the Copt, always eager to see that his property had not been stolen in the night, but early enough to share the first cup of tea of the day with the Tree's unwilling guardians.

'How much longer are we going to have to stay here?' asked one of his policemen.

'Not much longer, I think,' said Owen.

He took his cup of tea and walked over to where Daniel was looking at the names on the Tree and fretting at the diminishing rate of new inscriptions.

'If it goes on like this,' said the Copt gloomily, 'the Tree won't be worth having.'

'Have not the Belgians made you an offer?'

'That money is still to come, meanwhile, this lot has to be paid,' said Daniel, nodding sadly towards his Coptic henchmen.

'It could go on for ten years,' said Owen.

Daniel winced.

'Tell me, Daniel: every morning you ride here across the desert from Tel-el-Hasan, and every evening you ride home again. It must be a lonely ride, for there cannot be many who make the journey. You would remember those you saw. That night that Ibrahim died—'

'Would he had never died!' said Daniel gloomily. 'Since that day, the world has come to Matariya. If only it would go away again!'

'You remember the night? Well then, tell me, as you rode home to Tel-el-Hasan that night, did you meet anyone on the way?'

'I do not remember...'

'Think. They would have been coming from Tel-el-Hasan. Might you not have wondered why they were making the journey so late in the day?'

'That was not the riddle. He must have been taking her to meet her prospective husband's family. He would eat with the men and she with the women and then they would go home again. No, that was not the riddle.'

'What was the riddle, then?'

'That they should stay so late. For the next morning as I rode I saw them on their way back.'

'Ah! And their names?'

'It was Ali and his sister. You know, that mad brother of Leila's. Though who he was taking the girl to, I cannot think. For who, knowing what had happened to the husband of the one sister, would wish to take on the other sister and that mad family?'

'Thank you, Daniel.'

Owen rose from his squat. They would have to make inquiries but he was pretty sure that no prospective husband's family would be found. That was not what Ali and his sister had come over for. The old goatherd, as he had sat with his goats among the balsam trees by the well, had heard people talking by the Tree: a man and a woman. The sister had been there as bait. An assignation must have been made previously and Ibrahim, unable, it appeared, to resist any woman, and drawn to the sister anyway, had come to keep it.

But why had they taken so long? Some time must be allowed for them to take the body to the railway line and return; but then what had they been doing for the rest of the night? And why had they taken the body to the line anyway?

It kept coming back to that. And that, in fact, was where he, Owen, came in. For Ibrahim's murder was not, strictly speaking, the Mamur Zapt's concern but the Parquet's. Owen was interested only in so far as it impinged on wider issues, the progress of the new railway, for instance, and its political and commercial implications.

He still could not fathom that bit out. Was there a connection between Ibrahim's murder and the railway? Or were they quite separate, a matter of coincidence only, and Ibrahim's death merely another revenge killing, one of the many that swelled Egypt's crime lists?

One thing was clear, though. He had learned something that Mahmoud ought to know.

⟨⟩

'It's not enough,' said Mahmoud, however, as they walked away from the Tree the next morning, after Daniel had repeated his story for Mahmoud's benefit.

'Not enough? There won't be any family—'

'No, I know. But all that the Copt has told us is that Ali was in the area that night.'

'And his sister.'

'They might have gone on to somewhere else.'

'The goat man heard them. At the Tree.'

'We could still do with another witness.'

'We've already tried, but—'

Owen stopped.

'Wait a minute,' he said. 'I know somebody else who must have been near there that night. Or rather, something.'

'Something?' said Mahmoud.

⟨⟩

'Hello, Ja'affar,' said Owen. 'I'm surprised that you're not with your friend, the barber.'

'I'm just on my way,' said Ja'affar.

'My friend and I will walk with you if we may. How is the shoulder?'

'Getting better. Unfortunately.'

'Old man Zaghlul will soon be getting after you to go back, will he?'

'He's already been after me. In fact, he's after me most days.'

'Ah, well, there you are. You're such a good man that he needs you.'

'I'm beginning to wonder if I need him. It's those birds. Once they've given you something, you never feel quite the same about them again.'

'Ja'affar had his shoulder put out by one of the ostriches,' Owen explained to Mahmoud.

'They're like an express train,' said Ja'affar. 'They weigh a ton, and when they hit you, bang! Down you go and you're lucky if you don't get your back broken. You've got to be fit to handle those birds. At least, that's what I've been telling Zaghlul.'

'And what does he say?'

'He says you don't have to be fit just to carry food to them. That's true enough, but what happens if one escapes? You need every man you've got, then. And you need to be able to throw yourself around a bit, too. That's the bit I wouldn't fancy, not with a shoulder like this.'

'They're always getting out, are they?'

'It's the same one. When they've done it once, they know how to do it again. He's either going to have to put it in a special pen or shoot it. Pity Malik didn't shoot it the other day.'

'That was the one, was it?'

'It's always the same one.'

'And it's always getting out? You don't happen to remember, Ja'affar, do you, if it got out the night that Ibrahim was killed?'

'The night Ibrahim was killed? They came and told me about it at the farm. That was a day to remember! Everything was all over the place that morning. They had a job bringing it back, you see. There were only two of them, Zaghlul himself—how he found out it had gone, I don't know, I reckon he sleeps with those damned birds—and Sayid, who's on at nights. Just the two of them. Well, that's not enough, you need two just to handle the net, and then you need someone to chase it in. And at night, too! I don't know how they managed it.'

After what Ja'affar had said, they approached the ostrich farm with diffidence. It lay on the other side of the station at Matariya. The gap in the fence, broken on the day that Ja'affar had received his injury, had been repaired. There were ostriches on the other side, but perhaps, still mindful of the disturbance of the day, they were keeping to the far side of the pen.

Owen and Mahmoud had some way to walk before they found the entrance to the farm. It was not a place you would normally approach on foot, although, of course, the men who worked there did. For Owen and Mahmoud, unused to toiling across the desert in the heat, it was hard going.

The farm, out beyond the cultivated area surrounding the village, was desert not field. Desert was, presumably, what the ostriches were used to, although they may have preferred the grass of the south; and, of course, the land was cheap. The chief expense would have been the pens. The smaller ones were fenced off with wood, although wood itself, this near the city, was not cheap. In many places on the perimeter of the farm the wood had been replaced by cut thorn bushes, the traditional resource of the desert men; which explained, perhaps, why a determined ostrich was able to get out so regularly.

Zaghlul, they were informed, was out in the pens, which meant still more walking, some of it through the pens themselves. Owen was relieved to see that the ostriches kept away from them. On his way past some of the smaller pens he had been able to examine the birds closely. Up till now in his life he had never thought about ostriches. If asked, he would have said they were silly birds. They didn't fly, they just stood around awkwardly; their only use, so far as he could see, was to provide feathers for women's hats, which, although jolly, was hardly a crucial role in the modern economy; and with their small heads and their long necks and their general flapping about they seemed somehow scatty.

Now, however, viewed at close quarters and in the light of Ja'affar's words and experience, they appeared rather formidable.

They were, for a start, surprisingly tall, about nine feet. The small head had a sharp beak and the long neck looked as if it could deliver the beak with force and dexterity. The splendid feathers concealed a muscular body, and the feet—what was it that he had heard about the feet? Did ostriches kick? If they did, it looked as if it could prove a real finisher. Those feet, now: huge! And what about the claws? Equally long, and as sharp as the beak? On the whole he thought it best not to look too closely.

Wondering which to guard against, the feet or the beak, and deciding that probably the thing to worry about was being knocked over while he wondered, he reached the enclosure where Zaghlul was bent over a sick or injured ostrich being held on the ground by three men.

He saw them coming but ignored them. They stood politely waiting until he had finished doing whatever he was doing and the bird was released. One of the men helped it up. It stood for a moment as if shocked and then suddenly bolted away. For several minutes it ran frenziedly up and down the pen as if it had quite lost its senses. Zaghlul watched it for some time and then grunted, apparently with satisfaction.

Only then did he turn to Owen.

'Who's he?' he said, nodding at Mahmoud.

'The Parquet,' said Mahmoud.

'Ah, the Parquet.' Zaghlul had evidently heard of the Parquet. '*And* the Mamur Zapt,' he said after a moment.

'That's right. We want to ask you some questions.'

'The government would do better to listen than to ask questions,' said Zaghlul.

'We're ready to listen, too. And the first thing we want to listen to is why you told me that an ostrich had not escaped on the night Ibrahim was killed when it had.'

'Do I have to tell the government everything?'

'If you don't, it wonders why you can't.'

'There's no "can't" about it. I choose not to, that's all. I don't want to have anything to do with the government and I don't want the government to have anything to do with me.'

'That bit,' said Owen, 'you can't choose.'

'Have you something to fear?' asked Mahmoud.

'Fear?' said Zaghlul, frowning. 'What have I to fear?'

'You were there on the night that Ibrahim was killed.'

'I was somewhere on the night Ibrahim was killed.'

'You were by the Tree of the Virgin.'

Zaghlul was silent for a moment.

'Well,' he said, 'what if I was? I was following the bird. There's no crime in that.'

'A man was killed.'

'I did not kill him,' said Zaghlul.

'No?'

'No.'

'Who was with you?'

'No one was with me.'

'Sayid was with you. Be careful what you say. I shall speak with Sayid.'

'Sayid will say as I do. That I did not kill Ibrahim.'

'Who else did you see that night?'

'I saw no one.'

'Will Sayid say the same as you on that? If I go to him now and ask him?'

Zaghlul was silent for some time.

'I saw Ali,' he said at last, unwillingly.

'Of course you did. And his sister, too?'

'And his sister.'

'Tell me what you saw.'

'I will not tell you anything,' said Zaghlul, 'unless Ali bids me to.'

⚬ᴍᴍᴏ

'Was that Zaghlul I saw?' asked Ali, when they were sitting in the room used for the questioning of prisoners.

'It was.'

'What is he doing here?'

'He is here for the same reason that you are here.'

'That cannot be so.'

'If it cannot be so then you must tell us why it cannot be so.'

'Cannot Zaghlul tell you himself?'

'He says he will tell us nothing unless you bid him.'

They let him sit there for some time thinking this over. Then Owen said:

'He was there that night, wasn't he?'

'If he says so.'

'He does say so. He also says that he saw you. You and your sister.'

'Well, then.'

'You admit it?'

Ali shrugged.

'There is another who will say that you were in the area, too.'

'Well, then.'

The shrug this time had defeat in it. When, after a moment or two, he spoke, though, it was not about himself.

'Zaghlul here too?' He shook his head. 'He won't like that. He is a man of the open spaces.'

He seemed to have difficulty taking it in.

'Old man Zaghlul!'

After a while, Mahmoud prompted him.

'That night: tell us what happened.'

Ali jerked up with a start.

'That night? Oh, I helped him.'

'Helped him?' said Mahmoud and Owen together, taken aback.

'Yes. There were only two of them, you see. Well, that's not enough. You need at least three—one to drive, the other two to hold the net. Even that's not too many. They never run straight, you see. They're always twisting off to one side or the other. You've got to keep right behind them. And it's not easy in the dark.'

'You helped him catch the ostrich?'

'Yes. I knew about ostriches, see. I'd worked with him for a time on that farm of his. Just for a bit. I didn't stay long.

"This sort of thing's not for me," I said. "One of these days one of those bloody great things is going to peck my eye out." He tried to talk me round but I wouldn't have it. I wouldn't do it even for Zaghlul. He's always been good to me, you know. People say he's a mean old bastard, but he's always been all right with me. I used to work with him. Before he started up that ostrich farm.'

'Supplying the pilgrims?'

'Yes. First it was mounts, then it got wider. It looked pretty good to me, but Zaghlul said no, other people would come in. And when they started building this new town he said: "That's it!" So he sold up and off he went. He asked me to go with him. I was his right-hand man, you see. But the birds were not for me.'

'But you did lend a hand that night?'

'I could see he needed one. There was just him, you see, him and Sayid. I knew that wouldn't be enough, not in the dark. So I pitched in. It wasn't that easy even then. It took us the best part of the night. But in the end we did it. And it was only then, after we'd got the bird trussed up, that Zaghlul says to me: "Well, Ali, what are you doing here this time of night?"

"'I've had business to attend to," I says.

'And he says: "I reckon I saw some of that business back by the Tree. There's a dead man lying there."

"'I'm not saying anything," I says.

"'No," he says, "and you'd better not. But who was that girl, then?"

"'That was my sister," I says.

"'Oh," he says. Of course he knew the whole story. "Well," he says, "he had it coming to him."

'He was right, too. I couldn't do anything else, Leila being my sister. I was sorry in a way. He'd been a friend of mine. But I was that mad—! I'd brought them together, you see. I said to Ibrahim one day: "I've got a sister, you know." And he said: "Let's have a look at her, then." And it seemed all right. They're a good, hard-working family. But that stupid bastard—I ought to have known, all right. I ought to have known. But he was so open about it. Everyone knew about it. Well, I couldn't let that go on, could I? And then there was this other thing—it all came together, so he had to go, I couldn't do anything else, could I?'

'Why did you put the body on the line?' asked Mahmoud.

'That was Zaghlul's idea. "What are you going to do about that there body?" he says.

'"Leave it where it is," I says.

'"I've got a better idea than that," he says.

'"Oh?" I says. "What's that, then?"

'"Put it on that new railway line," he says. "That'll give them something to think about!"

'Well, the more I thought about it, the better I liked it. I reckoned Ibrahim wouldn't mind it at all. He's always been one to speak up against the Belgians and if he could cause them trouble just by lying there, I thought he'd be glad to. And then I knew how other people would see it. A death well spent, they would say. So I says, "Right, then."

'Well, old man Zaghlul helps me carry him—he weighed a bit, I can tell you, we had to drag him in parts—and we put him down there on the new railway line—all decent, mind you, quite respectful. And then I had to get away because it was already beginning to get light.'

~

Zaghlul confirmed the story, once he had received Ali's permission. So, too, did Sayid.

So also did Ali's sister, speaking to them in her brother's presence. The question arose of what to do with her. She was plainly an accomplice but equally plainly had been entirely under the influence of her brother, to whom it had obviously never occurred that if he were to suffer for the crime, she would suffer too.

'Effendi, this is not right!' he said to Owen, perturbed. 'She is a good girl.'

'Allowances will be made,' Owen assured him. 'I have spoken to my friend from the Parquet and he says that she will be treated lightly, the time she has served in prison being counted for her.'

'The time she has served in prison?' said Ali, aghast.

'Just until the trial.'

'How long will that be?'

'A month or two.'

Ali was still perturbed.

'Who will do the house?' he said.

'Have your brothers no wives?'

'No,' said Ali. 'For some reason families are not eager to marry us.'

'Well, that's your problem. Or your brothers'.'

They had been let out the day before.

'I will do what I can for her,' promised Owen.

And that, he thought with satisfaction, was that. The matter had been resolved, and without any of the wider problems, which had at one time seemed so threatening, coming to a head. In the end it had boiled down to another revenge killing, regrettable, but not, as he pointed out to Mr Rabbiki, exactly unusual in Egypt.

'The cause,' said Mr Rabbiki resourcefully, 'is the state of backwardness in which the people are kept. Now, with more education and more social spending—'

The Nationalists, however, dropped the issue like a hot brick. They had, in any case, got most of what they wanted. The government had been severely embarrassed. It had been shown, yet again, to be in the pocket of the foreigners. It would have been nice if the railway could have been delayed sufficiently to muck up the Khedive's plans for a Grand Official Opening, but you couldn't have everything. The Nationalists, anyway, were not against development. They were just against anyone else doing the developing.

The last part of the track was now being laid. A few things remained to be done but they would certainly be completed before the Opening. The Khedive purred like a contented cat.

The Belgians were already making arrangements to pull out. The Baron would retain a controlling interest in the New Heliopolis Scheme but from now on his influence would be able to be exerted from behind the scenes, which was likely to be less provocative and by no means less lucrative.

The Syndicate had had, in the end, nothing to do with the murder, Owen pointed out to Mahmoud as they sat sipping coffee one evening in a café in the Ataba. Nor, of course, as Mahmoud pointed out to Owen, had it had anything to do with the Nationalists. The Nationalists had, indeed, as Mr Rabbiki admitted privately, infiltrated Wahid among the railway workers so as to create trouble; but that trouble definitely did not extend to murdering Ibrahim. Wahid had been genuinely shocked and angered when the body had been found on the line. He had been convinced that it was the Syndicate's doing. That was why he had been so determined to make an issue of it.

By the time they had finished their second cup, Mahmoud had succeeded in convincing Owen that the Nationalist move had been fair, given the heavy-handedness of the Belgian employers; and by the time they had finished their third cup they had both agreed that the new electric railway and other such developments might actually be a good thing if the March of Progress eventually led to a diminution in the number of revenge killings in the more backward parts of Egypt.

Everything, thus, was tidied up. Except—

Except that one morning Ibrahim's widow, Leila, came to Owen. She sat down on the floor of his office, declining a chair; declining, too, the coffee he offered. He imagined that she had come to talk about the gratuity that he had persuaded the Syndicate to award her. He had asked for a pension but the Syndicate said that it did not pay pensions to widows, did not pay pensions anyway to casual workers, did not, in fact, if it could help it, pay pensions to anybody. A one-off cash payment in the circumstances and not to mar the Khedive's Official Opening, they were prepared to consider.

Leila had indeed come to talk about that. She was, first of all, astonished to receive anything. Having received it, though, she wanted to talk to Owen about the mechanics of the payment. Could it be done, she wondered, in such a way that the benefit would go to her children and not to the men of the family that she had married into?

Owen said that this was not easy, that if payment were made direct to the children then the family would simply annex it. Much the same would happen, he admitted, if the payment were made to her. The family would reason, he said, that since it was supporting her and her children, the payment should go to the common good.

That would be only fair, she said hesitantly. But suppose they were no longer supporting her?

What had she in mind, asked Owen.

What she had in mind, she said, was returning to the house of her brothers. They would be without a woman in the house now that her sister had gone with Ali into the *caracol.*

Ah, said Owen, but her sister would soon return. And would not her brothers do exactly the same as the men of her husband's family and take the money from her?

They would, she said; and therefore what she wanted was for Owen to keep the money for her and pay her a little each month which would go towards the general housekeeping. The rest would then be there should she and her children need it.

Owen said he thought he could do this and they spent some time discussing how the monthly payment might be made. She said the best thing might be for her to come to his office each month to collect it. Owen asked her how she proposed to travel to the city each time. It was, he knew, a big step for her. Indeed, it transpired that today was the first time she had actually been to the city. She had come on a cart. The lift had been arranged for her by the barber and some of Ibrahim's friends in Matariya. She thought that perhaps she could do the same again.

Owen said that she didn't have to come all the way to his office to collect the money. The payment could be made through the local mamur's office in Heliopolis.

Leila was silent for a moment or two. Then she said that she would prefer to come to the city as the local mamur was too much under the influence of the Pasha's son:

'And Malik has had too much to do with this business already.'

'In what way?'

Leila was silent now for quite some time. Eventually she said:

'He spoke to Ali.'

'Spoke to Ali?'

'My sister told me. He came over to the house one day and said he wanted to speak to Ali. They spoke for a long time. And afterwards Ali came back to the house and said: "Well, that is settled then."'

'And my sister asked what was it that was settled?'

'And Ali said it was no business of hers. And then he laughed and said that for once the Pasha's interests and his were the same. And then he thought, then looked at her, and said that perhaps it was her business after all.'

'She asked him what he meant and he said that she would find out soon enough. And then he would say no more.'

Owen thought for a moment.

'This was when? After Ibrahim and the Pasha's son had had hot words?'

'Yes. That kind of thing should not be,' said Leila bitterly. 'A Pasha and one of his villagers quarrelling over a slut! I said that to Ibrahim and he spoke to me roughly. So then I said it to my brothers. "A Pasha should not do such things," I said. "A Pasha can do what he likes," said Ali, "for he does it with his own. It is your husband that is at fault." Then I was silent, for I knew I would only make things worse between Ibrahim and my brother. Besides, I knew that Ali would take the Pasha's side.'

'Why would he do that?'

'He was one of the Pasha's men.'

'One of his villagers?'

'Not just that. He had done things for Malik. In the city. Along with others. And now they were all going to Heliopolis to work for him again!'

'Has Ali ever spoken to you the name Roukoz?'

'Yes.' Leila hesitated. 'But that was more in the past. He speaks a different name now.'

'What is that name?'

Leila looked him in the face.

'That of the local mamur,' she said.

Chapter 13

Owen had decided that the time had come to go riding. The following morning he rose early, as usual, borrowed a horse from the barracks at Abbasiya, and rode on out of the city in the direction of Heliopolis. This early in the morning riding was possible. Later, the heat would come up like a furnace and both man and horse would flinch. Out in the desert, which in those days began just out of town, the temperature would rise sharply. Only people used to it, like Zaghlul, would care to ride in the middle of the day.

But very early in the morning, when the sun was only just coming up, and the desert still had the freshness of the night, riding was not only possible but delightful. Owen, who had not ridden for some time, now wondered why he hadn't.

He put the horse into a gallop. It sniffed the air and responded strongly. The sun was still low in the sky, still retaining some of the redness, and their shadow stretched out forever across the sand.

There was no one else about. Over to his right he could see fields, but no villagers had yet come out to work in them. There, too, sharp against the sky, was the obelisk and somewhere over there would be the Tree.

He pressed on towards Heliopolis; and then suddenly he saw, away in the desert to the left of him, over towards the river, a solitary figure on a horse. It changed direction and came towards him.

While it was still some way away he saw that it wore jodhpurs, a sun helmet and, incongruously, a veil.

'Hello!' said Amina.

They began to ride along together.

'I wondered when you would come.'

'I would have come before but I've been rather preoccupied—'

'At five thirty in the morning?'

'Yes,' he said.

'With your fine lady?'

'With work. My day starts early.'

'And it is work that brings you here this morning?'

He smiled.

'Perhaps,' he said.

'Well, that is disappointing. Perhaps I shall go for a ride on my own.'

She galloped off. He followed her.

After a while she stopped.

'That *is* a relief!' she said. 'I was afraid for a moment you were not going to follow. At least you've been faithful so far. Or perhaps it is merely preoccupation with work?'

'That, too. I wanted to ask you something.'

'What do I get if I tell you?'

'What do you want?'

'You.'

'I'm afraid—' he began.

She nodded, accepting.

'You for a bit, then.'

'Well—'

It was not until later, fortunately, that he remembered how old she was, or, rather, wasn't. Then he reproved himself and rolled away.

Amina, too, however, had her preoccupations.

'I wish I was taller,' she said gloomily.

'What?' said Owen, startled.

'Like her.'

'Like—?'

'Your girlfriend. I saw her in the shop. She's Nuri Pasha's daughter, isn't she?'

'Yes. But tallness doesn't come into it.'

'I'm getting taller,' said Amina. 'It's just that it's taking a bit of time.'

'I wouldn't worry about that.'

'No,' said Amina, 'it's other things, isn't it?'

'The problem is,' said Owen, 'I'm faithful to her, too.'

'I know,' said Amina. 'Faithful everywhere. How difficult it must be!'

'You haven't hit it yet. It's like getting tall.'

'The fact is,' said Amina, 'I'm practising being unfaithful first.'

'Why are you practising being unfaithful?'

'Because if I ever marry Malik,' said Amina grimly, 'I'm going to be unfaithful all the time!'

'It might not come to that. Pashas' sons don't usually marry mamurs' daughters. Besides, whatever Malik might say, I don't think he intends—'

'It's not him,' said Amina. 'It's my father.'

'I know he wants to marry you well, but—'

'No, no. He knows something about Malik. Malik has to go along with him.'

'I wonder if it's the same thing as I know about Malik?'

Amina sighed.

'All right,' she said. 'I knew we would have to get round to it. What was it that you wanted to know?'

'The Racing Club at Heliopolis: what do you know about it?'

'It's controlled by a group of big men. The racing is only part of it. They're hoping to make the city a gambling centre in general. Casinos everywhere. The aim is to cater for the really rich. There are Pashas' palaces all round Heliopolis but it's not only them. They're looking further afield, abroad, even. They want people to come to Heliopolis just for the gambling. The racing is merely a sideshow, really, but it just happens to be the first part that's up and working.'

'What's the connection between them and the Syndicate?'

'There isn't one. The Belgians just build the facilities and let them out. Of course, they've a pretty good idea what they're going to be used for but they don't inquire too closely. There's too much money in it for them. Besides, the group has got influence. There are Pashas behind it. Royalty, even—'

'Is Malik a member of the group?'

'Not really. He's not clever enough or rich enough. But he thinks he is, and they let him go on thinking that. They use him to give evidence when they're applying for a licence to gamble, that sort of thing.'

'And other sorts of things?'

'Probably. He works with a man named Zenakis.'

'And your father?'

'They make use of him, too,' said Amina bitterly. 'He knows he's being used, of course, but he goes along with it because he thinks that's the way to get on. He wants to get on,' she said.

'I've noticed that. To the extent of marrying you off to Malik.'

'That's the bit,' said Amina, 'that I can't forgive.'

'I think,' said Owen, 'that I might be able to do something about that.'

⌀

'But, Ali,' said Owen, 'I am surprised: that a man like you, who used to go to hear the great Mustapha Kamil speak, should take the side of the Pashas.'

'He's my boss,' said Ali doggedly. 'There's got to be loyalty somewhere.'

'But to one such as Malik?'

'There's money in it, too.'

'You'd have done better to have stayed with old man Zaghlul and raised ostriches. I'll bet he wouldn't have taken the side of the Pashas.'

'He wouldn't that,' said Ali, chuckling.

'So why do you? Against your own people?'

'It's not my own people. We're just ripping off the rich.'

'Ah, but that's at Heliopolis. What about at Matariya?'

'We haven't done anything at Matariya.'

'No? What about killing Ibrahim?'

'That was a private matter.'

'What, then, had Malik to do with it?'

'His was a private matter, too.'

'If it was, why did he have to come to you? Could he not have settled it for himself?'

'It is not seemly for a Pasha's son to go around—'

Ali stopped.

'Killing people?' Owen finished for him. 'Is it more seemly, then, to do his dirty work for him? One villager to kill another? At the Pasha's behest?'

'I was going to kill him anyway.'

'Could he not wait? Was it that he had to make sure?'

'I don't know anything about all this,' said Ali. 'All I know is that he came to me and asked me when I was killing Ibrahim to put in a blow for him.'

'Would you have done it if he had not spoken?'

'Sure.'

'Even though Ibrahim was your friend?'

'He shamed us!'

'I'll bet,' said Owen, choosing his words carefully, 'that when Mustapha Kamil looked down and saw you standing in front of him, he would never have thought: there is a man who would kill his friend just because a Pasha says so!'

Ali jumped to his feet in fury.

Nationalism had its uses, thought Owen.

⁓

'You're not going to take a fellah's word against mine!' said Malik, shocked.

'Why not? Especially when there is corroborative evidence?'

'But he is just a rogue, a villain, a petty criminal!' Malik spluttered.

'That is so. And we shall show that you had criminal dealings with him.'

'Criminal dealings?'

'At the racetrack.'

'But that—But that—'

'Was just business?'

Malik went silent. After a moment he said:

'Ali would have killed him anyway.'

'True; and for that he will pay the price.'

'Quite rightly,' said Malik, recovering. 'A dangerous fellow.'

'But you had a hand in it. And for that you, too, must pay a price.'

'I don't think so,' said Malik confidently. 'For the death of a mere villager?'

'Perhaps not directly. Let us say, for your other dealings.'

'What price had you in mind?' asked Malik, amused.

'I think you should catch the next boat and stay out of Egypt for five years.'

'I'm afraid there's no chance of that. I have commitments here, you see.'

'I think the Racing Club might be prepared to release you.'

'I doubt that, actually. I'm much too valuable to them.'

'You could be in for a surprise.'

'And behind them there are even more powerful people.'

'The Khedive?'

Malik did not quite dare say that.

'Well, behind me,' said Owen, 'there is the Consul-General. So we'll just have to see.'

Who governed Egypt: the British Consul-General or the Khedive?

⟡

In fact, it was doubtful whether anyone governed Egypt; but in so far as the gambling laws were concerned, there was behind them a force greater than both the Consul-General and the Khedive: religious nonconformist opinion in England, which had recently returned a Liberal government for the first time in many years.

The Consul-General had already decided to tighten the gaming laws and refuse all new applications for licences, so when Owen went along and suggested that all was not as it might be in the New City of Pleasure it was very soon resolved that in future Heliopolis should seek its pleasure in other ways. The Consul-General's stance received strong support from the religious authorities in Egypt, both national and local, who pointed out the jarring proximity to the pilgrims' gathering place for the Mecca caravan; and also from the Nationalists, who felt that if the Khedive was for anything then there must be compelling reasons against it. Faced with such a coalition, the Pashas had little option other than to withdraw.

Withdrawal, of course, meant sacrifice, and one of the first sacrifices was Malik, who caught not the next boat but one very soon after it.

Another of the sacrifices was Salah-el-Din, who lost his post as mamur the day that Garvin heard about his links with the racetrack gang. Being an enterprising chap, he soon popped up again, but this time in Alexandria and in the private sector, where his foreign expertise and government contacts proved attractive to companies wishing to break into the Egyptian market. His contacts were not, perhaps, quite as good as they thought.

Owen was, on the whole, relieved, in view of what he had said to Amina, that Salah-el-Din did not decide to pursue his fortune abroad where he might have run into Malik and tried yet again to marry her off to him.

Amina did in the end make a good marriage; in fact, several of them.

When, during one of these, she was based for a time in Cairo, Owen caught sight of her occasionally. For the sake of peace and quiet he tried to keep this secret from Zeinab, usually without success, as her intelligence system was infinitely superior to his. She had, actually, nothing to fear, as he frequently pointed out to her. Zeinab, however, remained unconvinced. It was true that she still retained a decided advantage in height. Amina, though, was catching up rapidly in terms of maturity and experience; and then there was the troubling discrepancy in age. Zeinab watched Owen like a hawk.

Leila made the journey in each month from Tel-el-Hasan to draw her money from Owen's office. She was needed less at her brother's house now that her sister had been released, and one day she shyly mentioned the growing warmth of her relationship with one of Ibrahim's friends.

Owen took the hint and the next time he dropped in on the barber's circle at Matariya took the opportunity to praise her virtues; not least among which was her possession of a nest-egg securely lodged with the Mamur Zapt.

The barber's friends rejoiced at his good fortune.

'The love of a good woman is beyond the price of rubies,' he said. 'However, if she has some rubies as well, it is even better.'

It would go some way towards compensating for the collapse of his other prospects. The Racing Club, it seemed, was no longer interested in purchasing land for gallops. Despite this, he remained committed to Progress.

'One day,' he prophesied, 'there will be houses from here to Cairo! And the pilgrims will go to Mecca not by camel, no, nor even by train; but by flying carpets which will take them up and carry them to Mecca in the blink of an eye!'

The whole circle—and Owen—united in declaring this to be a load of utter bollocks. However, a future historian might interpose that some eighty or ninety years later this was, in a way, precisely what did happen.

To receive a free catalog of other Poisoned Pen Press titles, please contact us in one of the following ways:

Phone: 1-800-421-3976
Facsimile: 1-480-949-1707
Email: info@poisonedpenpress.com
Website: www.poisonedpenpress.com

Poisoned Pen Press
6962 E. First Ave. Ste 103
Scottsdale, AZ 85251